Copyright © 2024 Kate Yazowski

All rights reserved

The characters and events portrayed in this book are fictitious. Any similarity to real persons, living or dead, is coincidental and not intended by the author.

No part of this book may be reproduced, or stored in a retrieval system, or transmitted in any form or by any means, electronic, mechanical, photocopying, recording, or otherwise, without express written permission of the publisher.

ISBN 9798337664385

Cover design by: Art Painter
Library of Congress Control Number: 2018675309
Printed in the United States of America

Heaven's Deadly Valentine

by:

Kate Yazowski

Copywrite Kate Yazowski 2024

PROLOG

On a warm January day, I stood on the sidewalk holding onto my sister's ankles while she replaced lights in our outdoor sign. Inside there was an enormous pile of boxes to be unpacked, inventoried, and put on display for our second biggest holiday. Valentine's Day in Heaven was almost as profitable as Christmas. This year we were also waiting for the new candy sweet shop that was scheduled to open the week before the holiday. It was always exciting when a new business opened in our town.

Heaven hadn't had a good sweet shop in many years and from the promotional advertising, Sandy's Sweet Sensations were going to be exceptional. The brains behind the shop belonged Sandy Jessop. She was new to the community, having moved here from the New York City area. There, she had managed a very successful bakery and chocolate business. Sandy was friendly and outgoing, and seemed to fit into our community quickly. She had leased a small space that had been vacant for a while.

Soon we were all intrigued about what the shop would bring to our ever curious taste buds. Hattie had joined us on the sidewalk and stood staring up at the sign as Helen worked at replacing the bulbs. Hattie Beasley owns the bookstore right next to the Two Sisters Gift Shop. She's spunky, smart, and knows just about everyone in Heaven. We had become close to her ever since Helen had opened the shop nearly four years earlier.

Just down the street, three doors from the new sweet shop Mark

Harrison had opened his shop after the fire had destroyed the old one. Mark grew up here and, like Hattie, knows or has an opinion just about everyone. Small towns, build strong relationships in the business community and Heaven was no exception. The town had been through some rough patches the past year. A murder that uncovered a major drug lab and the revenge killing of Santa on the Holidays. Still, the town welcomed everyone with open arms. Little did we know that sometimes something sweet is also something deadly. With the last bulb in place, Helen returned to the sidewalk and folded the ladder.

"Looks better," she announced as Hattie and I followed her back inside. "Would you like a cup of coffee?" I asked Hattie as we made our way through the shop to the office area. "No time, but thanks," Hattie replied.

"Just stopped over to see if either of you were going to attend the pre opening of the candy shop tomorrow?" "I think we can wait a few more days." Helen replied as she surveyed the pile of boxes awaiting our attention.

"I think I'm going to stop over and see what it's all about," Hattie said. "Besides, they are advertising free chocolates." She smiled. "I'll bring you girls a couple of pieces." She added and headed for the door.

If there was just a clue about what was about to happen, then possibly we could have prevented it. Instead, we went about opening and inventorying the new merchandise blissfully unaware of the future.

CHAPTER 1

The pre-opening celebration at Sandy's Sweet Sensations was, by any definition, a success. Everyone who had any taste for chocolate lined up to sample the locally made confections. The brightly polished glass display cases gleamed. The assortment of candy, muffins, sweet breads and cakes was impressive and reminded many of the big city bakeries.

Hattie was bubbling with excitement as she delivered a small box with six of the most delightful looking candies I had ever laid eyes on.

"You just have to try these!" Hattie announced. "They are absolutely the best I have ever tasted!"

The gold lined box contained four chocolates. Three remained as Hattie had already sampled. Helen and I each made a selection.

 I bit into the dark chocolate, and instantly a burst of strawberry filled my mouth. I had eaten my share of chocolates, but this sensation was different and begged for seconds. Helen swallowed and shook her head. "Hattie, these are fantastic!" she said. "That was amazing!"

Hattie nodded in agreement. "She's giving a sample box away today and tomorrow. Then open for business!" As Hattie left the shop, our mouths were watering for more. And. I planned on stopping by the shop at lunchtime for a sample box.

We spent the day unpacking and taking inventory of the new Valentine merchandise, with a few customers coming in. It surprised me to see that most people had visited the new chocolate store and sampled various items. I grabbed our lunch at the Sub store and checked out the Sweet Shoppe. I selected a box from the table and surveyed the display cases of chocolates, muffins, and cakes. Everything was all perfectly aligned and looking delicious.

By closing time, we had updated the inventory and unpacked and displayed all the new merchandise. We had eagerly devoured the sample box of chocolates. Helen and I had decided we'd stop at Stu's for burgers and some wine. Stu's is a landmark in Heaven and besides being a lively bar, they have good food and a relaxed atmosphere.

No booths were available, so we seated ourselves at a small table in front of the bar. There was a mix of regulars and tourists enjoying the jukebox and conversation. Our burgers arrived, and we sat taking our time and enjoying the early evening crowd.

Sandy Jessops appearance in Stu's stopped just about every conversation in the room. She captivated the room in a black cocktail dress, catching everyone's attention. The outfit was big city, high society and on the top side of sexy. We followed as she passed our table and joined a well-dressed man seated in one of the back booths.

A rumble of whispered comments rippled through the bar before regular conversation resumed.

"Now, that's one hot chocolatier," Helen said with a chuckle.

I agreed. "The men in this town will beat a path to that shop." I commented with a chuckle. When we left to go home, Sandy

Jessop and her male companion were still at Stu's and still the subject of hushed conversation.

CHAPTER 2

It was a week before Valentine's Day that Sandy's Sensational Sweet Shop had opened officially. The good citizens of Heaven lined up to get the free red heart that held twenty pieces of Sandy's chocolates. You got the heart box free with any fifteen dollar purchase.

I visited the shop on its second day for a sweet snack after lunch. The line was long, but I finally got four double chocolate brownies and the free candy heart. Back at the shop, Helen and I shared one brownie and set the rest aside for dinner and tomorrow.

The heart-shaped box wrapped in red cellophane and finished with a gold ribbon and bow. It was an ideal gift for any Valentine. We decided that we'd save the box for another day. Hattie and Mark both had been to the shop and purchased items sufficient to get their free box.

Hattie had opened it and came into the shop late in the afternoon to share the luscious sweets inside. The following day, the morning paper reported a suspicious death of a young woman in Harris. She had died suddenly after suffering what appeared to be a heart attack in her home. Helen and I both read the article and commented on how sad it was for a young person to die.

At ten o'clock, our shop was open and Mark and Hattie had joined us for coffee and cinnamon buns from Sandy's shop. As with everything else we had sampled, they were delicious and hit the right combination of sweet and cinnamon.

We were busy for the rest of the morning with last minute Valentine shoppers and by lunch time ready for sandwiches and milkshakes. Helen made the run to the deli and noticed the line at Sandy's shop was longer than it had been the day before.

Shelia Whitmore picked up a cake and a free box of chocolate and crossed the street to shop for a gift for her husband. Shelia was the head teller at the bank and loved to browse our shop for gifts.

"Hey girls," she announced as she entered the shop. "Got to find something special for hubby Marty," she said and dropped her bakery bag on the floor by the cash stand. "I think something for his desk." She added and made her way toward the back, where we displayed desk sets and pens.

She made her selection and returned to the cash stand. "Have you tried the chocolate at Sandy's?" she asked. We both acknowledged that we had, and the candy was exceptional. "She sure is a popular item around town." Shelia remarked as Helen wrapped the pencil set.

"We know." I replied. "She was in Stu's the other night looking like a high end call girl."

"Baby, if you've got it, flaunt it." Shelia said, "And that woman has it." We laughed. as Shelia picked up the bakery bag and our gift bag. "Well, ladies, I'm going home and break into this heart. Maybe I'll get lucky and Marty will get one for tomorrow." She smiled and opened the door. "Later!" she called as it closed behind her.

Derrek leaned back in his office chair and studied the catalog of ladies' clothing. His girlfriend Trish loved nice lingerie, and this company had the best teddy sets. He'd have to order it now as the company delivered within twenty-four hours, which would be perfect..

Just as he was about to reach for the phone. Officer McClusky opened the door. "Chief, we're needed at the Whitmore residence ASAP. Marty Whitmore just found his wife dead."

Shelia Whitmore's body lay on the kitchen floor. She had obviously died suddenly, as there had been no attempt to call for help. On the table was a cake box still tied with string, a gift bag from Two Sisters, and a red heart of chocolate with three pieces missing.

There was no sign that an intruder had been in the house, and nothing was missing. Shelia's purse lay on the table and had plenty of cash and credit cards still in her wallet.

Marty Whitmore sat on the porch swing with head in his hands sobbing. "I came home and there she was on the floor. I checked for a pulse and there was none, so I called you and came out here," he sobbed as Derrek sat down beside him.

"Was she having any health issues?" Derrek asked, as the coroner's van pulled into the driveway. A second Heaven squad car had been called to keep the neighbors and others back away from the house.

Dr. Johnson kneeled down beside the body and studied its position and coloring. "She definitely had a violent death," he remarked, noting the obvious position of the body. "Based on my initial observation," Dr. Johnson remarked, "it appears someone poisoned her."

Paul Mc Clusky slid an evidence bag over the heart-shaped box. He also bagged the half-eaten sandwich and bag of chips that were on the table. "If it's something she ate, we'll have a good chance it was something here on the table." He said. Dr. Johnson took the bagged items and slid them into a brown paper bag, setting the bag on the gurney beside the body.

The Chief asked Marty Whitmore to wait in his car down the street to prevent him from seeing what was happening in his kitchen. They planned to take him to the station for some routine questions. Derrek joined McClusky in the kitchen and surveyed the room. Except for the items on the table, it was clean and everything seemed in order.

"Doc Johnson suspects poison. I bagged the food on the table and he took it for testing."

Derrek nodded "Good work Paul" he said, taking a deep breath. "The hard part is going to be finding out how," he added and made his way to the street and his squad. Marty sat in the back, still sobbing.

"You okay to answer a few questions?" Derrek asked, sliding behind the wheel.

"I think so," Marty answered as the car pulled away from the curb.

For the next few hours, Derrek went step by step through Shelia's day. Marty had composed himself and sat with both hands gripping a mug of coffee that shook as he held it.

"We had breakfast around seven," he said, taking a sip of coffee. "Normal eggs and toast and coffee," he added.

"I left for work about eight and she was going to get dressed and do the shopping." His voice trembled, and he blinked back tears.

"I talked to her at lunchtime and she was perfectly fine," he added. "Perfectly fine.

Derrek laid his pen down on the notepad. "Marty, this is important. Did she mention where she was going to shop?

Marty shook his head. "I'm sorry, she may have, but I don't remember. "

With that, he burst out in tears and put his hands over his face.

"I'll be back in a few minutes." Derrek said, standing and opening the door.

Outside, he found Paul McClusky at his desk and on the phone. He raised a finger as Derrek approached and ended the conversation.

"Dr. Johnson assures me he'll have preliminary results by noon tomorrow, confirming the poisoning, without a doubt.

Derrek nodded. "Marty is in pretty terrible shape. I don't think he has any family here, so how about you take him over to the hotel and get him a room?"

McClusky nodded and headed back to the interrogation room. A moment later, both he and Marty Whitmore made their way out the door.

CHAPTER 3

Hattie was so upset that her entire body shook. She was sitting in the back room of our shop with a mug of coffee and an oversized slice of carrot cake from Sandy's shop. "I'm telling you, it's just a matter of time." She said sharply.

"You know how this town is, and it's just a matter of time before the powers that be force that woman to leave town. Most likely on a rail," she added.

Helen sat on a chair beside her with a puzzled look on her face. It was fifteen minutes until we opened and Hattie had been rattling on for nearly half an hour. "Hattie, what are you getting at?" Helen asked for the third time. "Why would anyone want to run Sandy out of town?"

Hattie stopped and blinked. "Did you hear? Don't you know?" she asked.

"Apparently not." Helen replied. "So why don't you tell us?"

"It's all over town!" Hattie proclaimed loudly. "Ever since she walked into Stu's looking like a big city hooker!" Helen and I exchanged glances while suppressing a smile.

"We were there Hattie." I said. "She dressed a bit provocatively, but I don't see the connection," I said.

Hattie shook her head. "You girls need to get on the mainstream of talk," she announced. "Some of the local women are already talking about meeting with her and, as they say, 'setting her straight'."

I couldn't help but giggle. "Should she dress like a quaker?" I asked

Hattie made a face and got to her feet. "I'm telling you they are going to run her out of town if she shows up anywhere looking like that again." and with that she made for the door.

As it shut behind her, we both burst out laughing. "Sounds as if there might be ladies in town that don't like competition for their man's attention." Helen said, still smirking.

I glanced out the window at the shop, which even at ten in the morning had a line down the sidewalk. "Maybe they are worried about what Sandy makes that is so sensational?" I asked as Helen flipped the open sign and unlocked the front door.

Derrek reread the autopsy report on Shelia Whitmore. His eyes traveled to the face of Dr. Johnson and held, "So you found strychnine in her body?" He asked.

Johnson nodded. "In large enough quantities to kill within half an hour. And we also found large amounts in other chocolates in the Valentine box she had opened,"

"So the candy killed her?" Derrek asked, without expecting an answer.

Dr. Johnson got to his feet. "There is no question it killed her and the candy contained it. So, you've got a solid case of murder on your hands, Chief." He opened the office and turned back to the Chief. "I'd have a talk with that lady at the candy shop ASAP." he added and was gone.

Sandy was filling an order for two dozen cupcakes when

Derrek walked in, pushing past the line of people waiting. She acknowledged him with a nod and continued on to the next customer.

On the side wall, by the cake display, was a table piled high with red candy hearts. A sign announcing the box was free with any fifteen dollar purchase. Derrek made his way to the table, picked up a box at random, and laid a ten and five-dollar bill on the counter. "I'll just take this and be on my way," he said to Sandy, who nodded, scowled and went back to filling customers' orders.

An hour later, he had delivered the box to the lab for testing and was back in the office checking the background of one Sandra Jean Jessop.

Sandy was born in Del Mar, where she had lived until attending grade school. The family relocated to Harris and she graduated from high school there. She had a college degree in business and a culinary degree from a top rated university. Sandy had moved to New York City, where she had opened a small candy store, and over the five years there, she had prospered as the business grew. Seeking life away from the big city, she had returned to Harris briefly before moving to Heaven and opening Sandy's Sweet Sensations.

She had no criminal record, not even a parking ticket. But she had three failed relationships with men while in New York. All three were wealthy entrepreneurs and well seated in society. It was unclear why the relationships had failed, but Derrek noted the names and planned to follow up with checks on all three.

Peter Robinson had spent most of his college years dating Sandy Jessop. He had also worked with her in the New York City Candy store. After Sandy moved back to Harris, the relationship cooled and Peter found a job as a pastry chef at one of New York's finer hotels. He had three minor brushes with the law, all related to driving under the influence. Nothing else was of note in his history. Derrek noted the name and phone number of Peter's employer, along with the address listed as Robinson's current address.

Todd Keller apparently dated Sandy at the same time as Peter Robinson. Keller was best described as a player. He inherited a sizable trust fund from his father's business and spent his life bar hopping and clubbing at some of the top places in and around Manhattan. There was nothing listed as employment, no sign he had ever had a brush with law enforcement, and his current residence was unknown.

Randy Collins was the third known New York social connection. He was an up-and-coming Wall Street investor and hedge fund manager. Randy played the field and apparently paid a lot of attention to women of means and beauty. Apparently, he had made a small one time loan to Sandy when she was opening the New York City location. She repaid the loan after eight months, and the two dated casually off and on for the next couple of years. He had a clean record, and the current address in New York was worth what ten homes in Heaven would be.

As Derrek scanned the information, it didn't seem there was anything pointing to a former companion being current in her life or having had contact with her for years. The Sweet Shop closed at six, so Derrek sent Paul McClusky over to escort Miss Jessop to the station for a conversation.

It was a little after four in the afternoon and Becky Wright was tired and depressed. It had been a frightful day at work. Her feet ached and her back hurt as she landed with a thud on the living room sofa. The red candy heart caught her eye. She had picked it up when purchasing doughnuts for the office. Now she studied it and wondered how many calories would be in just a couple of pieces. After all, she could always spend an extra hour at the gym to work off any extra calories. Twenty minutes later, Becky Wright was lying on the floor of her living room. Her body contorted from the violent seizures. A piece of chocolate fell from her hand and rolled a few feet on the floor, coming to rest at the edge of the shag rug. A co-worker who came to pick her up for work would find her body around seven in the morning.

The second death of a Heaven resident found with a heart-shaped box of chocolates from Sandy's shop set the town on fire.

Derrek was pacing back and forth in the interrogation room, waiting for Officer McClusky to return with Sandy Jessop.

Laying on the long oak table were two autopsies reports. Shelia Whitmore and Becky Wright had died of strychnine poisoning and the candy had apparently come for the chocolate hearts sold at Sandy's Sweet Sensations.

Sandy Jessop entered the interrogation room and locked eyes on Derrek. "Chief, what exactly is this all about?" she asked.

"Take a seat." Derrek replied, motioning toward the table. Sandy pulled out the nearest chair and sat, placing both hands on the table.

"I don't understand why I'm here." She said, maintaining eye contact with Derrek.

Nodding, Derrek slid both autopsy reports over in front of her. "You're here because of these," he said flatly, taking a seat opposite her.

Sandy picked up the reports and scanned the pages. Her eyes going wide and her face going pale.

"You think I did this?" she asked, unable to control the shaking of her voice.

"Didn't you?" Derrek asked,

"My God, NO!" she exclaimed. "Why would I poison customers I don't even know? Why would I put everything on the line?" she let the reports slide from her hands

"I don't understand any of this," she said firmly.

"Neither do I." Derrek replied.

"Here's what I know. These two women died of strychnine poison from chocolate that came from the boxes of Valentine candy in your shop. We found other pieces of chocolate in these boxes that contained the poison."

Sandy shook her head. "I don't understand."

Derrek took a deep breath. "Tell me about the chocolates in those boxes. Do make them in the shop?"

Sandy shook her head. "I make most of them, but not all."

"Now I don't understand." Derrek said.

Sandy took a deep breath. "I'm in the process of purchasing some equipment."

"I purchase the hard creams and the jelly centers."

"From where?" Derrek asked, flipping open his notepad.

"A candy company in New York City. It's called Elegant Design Sweets" Sandy shook her head. "I can't believe any of this." She was about to continue when the door opened.

"Sorry Chief" Sally Collins said "There's been another murder. Officer Tim Hailey just called it in."

"Where?" Derrek said, getting to his feet.

"Kathleen Johnson, at her house on Wilson Street," Sally said.

"You can go for now," Derrek said to Sandy. "But you best pull those free hearts."

Sandy stood and walked to the door. "I'll do it right now," she replied and vanished down the hallway.

Kathleen Johnson lay on the floor of her living room. The poison had done its job, contorting her body badly from a seizure.

Officer Tim Hailey was standing in the doorway as Derrek's car screeched to a halt.

"She's in the living room, Chief. Mailman found her. Had a certified letter. She didn't answer the bell, and he saw her body through the window. "Hailey explained.

"Thanks Tim." Derrek said, clapping his hand on the officer's shoulder. "I called Dr. Johnson," Hailey added. "Should be here anytime now."

Derrek nodded and made his way to the living room where the body lay.

There on the coffee table was an open box of candy. The lid from the heart box had tumbled to the floor along with several pieces of candy. A piece was still in Kathleen's hand.

Dr. Johnson cleared his throat." Got another one," he remarked as he entered the room.

"It would appear so," Derrek replied. "There's an unknown number of boxes that were given away. No telling how many more are out there."

Johnson shook his head. "Crime scene unit will be here in a few," he said, making his way to the body. "We'll take it from here, Cheif." he added.

Derrek nodded. "I'll be at the sweet shop," he added and made his way outside.

"Stay with it, Tim. Leave your report on my desk."

"Sure thing, Cheif." Hailey replied as the crime scene unit pulled into the driveway.

Hattie charged into the shop and blurted out, "There's another body."

Several customers turned toward her and stared.

"I'm sorry." Hattie said quickly as both Helen and I started toward the front of the shop.

Hattie quickly made her way to the back office while we tended to the customers and reassured them that Hattie was referring to the local playhouse.

While Helen was finishing the last customer, I made my way to the back.

Hattie was sitting on the corner of the desk, her face pale and her hands trembling.

"Kathy, don't eat any of that candy," she announced as I entered. "It's poison!"

"Hattie! Slow down and take a deep breath!" Helen said sharply

"I just found out that there are three people dead, and they were all poisoned by that chocolate heart!" Hattie stammered.

"I just told Mark not to touch it. And I put mine in the trash!" She gulped in air and took several deep breaths. "It's on the news that they just found Kathleen Johnson dead at home!"

Helen and I exchanged glances. I glanced to the front and could see that there were no customers on the sidewalk in front of the sweet shop. The window sign read "CLOSED"

"So Sandy is poisoning people by giving them free candy?" I asked. "That just makes no sense. "

Just then, a tap came on the front door and we could see Mark standing outside. I went to let him in while Helen made hot tea.

"Oh, she's here!" Mark announced as he reached the back room and saw Hattie perched on the corner of our desk.

"What is going on?" Helen asked. "Hattie, you scared those customers. So what the heck is this about?"

"Helen, I'm sorry. Please forgive me, but there are at least three people who have died from those chocolates!"

"What?" Helen exclaimed.

"There is poison in some of the candy and it kills. I just heard that they found Kathleen Johnson dead on her living room floor. She still had a piece of candy in her hand!" Mark announced. "I think we should take all our boxes to the police."

Helen shook her head. "So the owner or someone at the sweet shop is putting poison in the candy and killing people at random?" She looked back and forth between Hattie and Mark. "You realise that makes no sense?"

Hattie studied her feet and shrugged. "It may not make sense, but it's happening."

"What would be her motive?" I asked. "She is new in town, so it can't be a grudge. She's new to business, so why risk all that investment?"

"Well, the people are dead." Mark said firmly. "So if the candy is poison, then it's got to be her."

I shook my head. "Helen is right. It makes no sense."

"Well, don't eat that candy!" Hattie exclaimed. She turned to Mark, "And that goes for you too!'

With that, she got to her feet and headed to the door. Mark followed. Helen and I exchanged glances and made our way back to the front.

"What do you make of that?" I asked, pointing across the street. A squad car had parked in front of the sweet shop and a large van from the crime lab was unloading equipment onto the sidewalk.

"It's going to ruin her business." Helen said. "It just makes no sense for her to do something like this."

"What about someone doing it to her?" I asked.

CHAPTER 4

Stu's was buzzing when we entered around six thirty. News had traveled fast and where the facts were missing, fantasy and gossip would do.

We had just started our cheeseburger plates when the door opened and Sandy Jessup walked in. She looked haggard and pale. Her eyes scanned the room for a table. The conversations stopped and an awkward silence filled the bar.

Helen waved a hand, motioning to the empty seat at our table. A moment later Sandy slid in and mouthed "thank you."

Emily, the waitress, approached the table. "Want something?" she asked Sandy.

"She'll have a cheeseburger plate and a glass of house wine." Helen said. "And put it on our bill," she added.

"You don't have to buy me dinner." Sandy said. "It's been a bad day and I appreciate your kindness." She added.

"Want to talk about it?" I asked

Sandy shrugged. "I don't know where to start." the wine arrived, and she took a deep swallow.

The police are going through all the candy in my shop looking for strychnine." She paused while Emily delivered her burger.

"Strychnine?" Helen asked. "That's an old heart medication that isn't used any longer. It's safe in small quantiles but lethal in larger doses."

"Exactly," Sandy replied as she poked french fries around on the plate.

They are going through every damn piece of chocolate in the place. Not only the Valentine Heart's but also the cases as well. They could arrest me any minute.

"Listen, don't just give up." Helen said. "Chief Landly is fair, and if you didn't do it, you'll be fine."

She swallowed hard. "And what about the business? People won't buy from someone they think poisoned them?"

She scrubbed her cheeks with the back of her hand. "I have invested every penny I have in that shop. Every last cent." She said and pushed her plate away without touching it.

"I appreciate your kindness." She said and got to her feet.

"Good night." She added and hurried to the door.

"Now what?" I asked as Helen took a deep breath and leaned back in the booth.

"We help find out who is behind this," she said and signaled to Emily for the check.

Derrek seated himself behind the desk and motioned to the chairs.

"How can I help you ladies?" he asked.

"We'd like to help find whoever is behind this poison candy." Helen said. "I don't think that Sandy Jessop is the one responsible."

Derrek allowed a small smile to cross his face.

"I agree," he said. "But exactly how can you help when we don't have a clue?"

"Because we're not you." Helen replied. "People will say things to us they wouldn't say to you and frankly, we can go places where you can't."

"Such as?" Derrek asked.

"Such as the spouses and relatives of the victims. We can scope out things that might not surface in your official investigation."

Derrek nodded." And that leaves me to come to your rescue when you get yourselves into trouble?"

"No trouble Chief." I added quickly.

The room went silent for a moment. Derrek studying us and we studying him in return.

"Okay." he said slowly, "But you better keep your noses clean doing this," he added.

"As clean as possible." Helen said, smiling

Derrek opened the folder in front of him and scanned the page. "We have three deaths linked to the candy hearts that were given away," he said.

"All local, all unconnected, as far as we can tell."

"There could be others?" Helen asked.

"There could be people on tourist buses, people from other parts of the state. There is no way to tell."

"We've found 17 more hearts in the shop that contain three or more pieces containing poison," he added.

"And are there certain pieces in every box that were poisoned, or does it vary?" Helen asked.

"It's mostly the same type of chocolate that has been involved. According to Sandy, she purchased these chocolates from a wholesale house called Elegant Design Sweets. It is a large wholesale house in New York City.

Helen thought for a moment. "So none of the locally made chocolate contained the poison?" she asked.

"We don't know that for sure, but the boxes we took from the shop that had poison were the same pieces that were purchased from the New York wholesale house."

He leaned back in his chair. "We've contacted them and they immediately referred us to their corporate attorney." He took a deep breath. "I doubt we'll get much from them."

Helen nodded. "Okay Chief, we'll do some poking around locally." she got to her feet. "Sandy didn't do this, but whoever did is out to ruin her."

Derrek nodded. "She's in the clear with my department for now. I told her she can re-open today." Helen smiled. "We'll be in touch." and she headed for the door with me in tow.

We opened the gift store for the day and invited both Hattie and Mark over for coffee at lunchtime. In between customers, I made a list of the three local victims and what we knew about them.

Shelia Whitmore was the head teller at the local bank. She was married to Marty Whitmore, one of the top real estate brokers in the area. While Shelia had no apparent enemies and was well liked and friendly, Marty might perceive things differently.

As a broker, he had been involved in some of the most impactful transactions in the village. There were several clients from out of the area that he had represented while they attempted to buy property for large corporations. Heaven was extremely closed minded to outside development and there was a good amount of controversy about the deals at the time. They all were unsuccessful and Marty lost a lot of commission money on them. He was, to say the least, unhappy about those losses and made no attempt at hiding how he felt.

Becky Wright was a young cashier at the local food market. She was friendly and got along with just about everyone. Becky dated a lot of different men and didn't care if they were single, married or divorced. A year back, she had gotten into a nasty scandal when a local man by the name of Andy Schaffer lead her on for several weeks. Mrs. Andy Schaffer found out about the affair and threatened Becky with some nasty physical payback. It was a safe conclusion that there were others in the area who had a reason not to like her.

Kathleen Johnson was a middle-aged grandmother with grown children outside the Heaven area. She was a retired schoolteacher and a widow. From everything we knew about her, she was a good neighbor, went to church on Sunday and kept to herself most of the time. There wasn't anything that either of us could think of that would prompt someone to kill her.

Mid morning, I went across the street to the sweet shop to talk to Sandy. I found her behind the counter, sitting on a stool.

She smiled when I entered and asked for a half dozen brownies. "Poisoned or plain?" she asked as she placed them in a box.

"Listen, we've gotten the permission from the Chief to snoop around and try to figure this out." I said, handing her the money. "Do you know any of the ladies who died?" I asked.

She shook her head. "No, so many people came in here and bought stuff. I can't say that I know anybody other than to recognize their faces if they come back in.

"Try not to worry." I told her, picking up the box of brownies. "We'll figure this out."

She feigned a smile and returned to her stool. "I just hope I can hang on that long," she whispered as I closed the door.

Mark, Hattie, Helen, and I sat with mugs of coffee and the box of brownies in the back of our shop.

"Are these things safe?" Mark asked before picking one up to eat.

"Of course!" Helen snapped. "Sandy didn't do this," she added.

Hattie's eyebrows shot up. "Then who did?" she asked, placing a brownie on a napkin.

"We had a long talk with Derrek." Helen said." The department doesn't think she's responsible."

"What does that mean?" Mark asked. "The candy came from her shop. So if not her, an employee?"

"We'll need to check the three people that work there. But, the pieces that have the poison came from a wholesale candy maker called Elegant Design Sweets, in New York City."

Mark chewed a mouthful of brownie and swallowed. "Why would they sell poison sweets?" he asked." Does she have a connection with them?"

"Unknown." I said. "The company has referred Derrek to their attorney, so who knows when or if they will even respond or cooperate?"

"If we don't find the real person or persons responsible for this, Sandy Jessop is going to lose everything." Helen said.

"She told us she has invested every penny into that shop and if people think she poisoned people, she'll lose it all." I added.

"Then we better figure this out." Hattie said firmly. "It's the least we can do if she's innocent."

Mark nodded in agreement. "I agree," he said. "Where do we start?"

CHAPTER 5

Derrek was on hold. He tapped his pencil on the desk blotter and studied a small spider weaving a web outside his office window. He had been on hold for nearly ten minutes.

After a check with the New York City Police he'd learned there were no legal problems with Elegant Design Sweets, he had placed a call directly to the company.

They had shuffled him to three different extensions, and now he was holding for the President of Public Affairs.

"Good Morning, this is Andrew Lawson. How may I assist you?" a male voice said briskly into the receiver.

"Good Morning Mr. Lawson, Chief Landly of the Heaven Police Department."

"Excuse me, did you say Heaven?" came the reply.

"I said Heaven." Derrek said, "I'm calling about an issue we have here that involves some of your products that were purchased by Sandy's Sensational Sweets, Sandra Jessop."

"I'm sorry, but I'm not familiar with that account," Lawson replied. "Shall I pull the file?"

"Yes please, I'll hold." Derrek tapped his pencil harder.

"One moment." the line went dead and soothing music with a woman's voice describing the line of cream filled chocolate the company sold.

"Ok, I have the file." Lawson returned to the line. "A small account started about 6 weeks ago. One order placed and shipped." He added.

"Could you tell me what was on the order?" Derrek asked.

"Looks like jelly centers, assortment twenty and hard creams assortment eighty four. One shipment of 250 pieces each." Lawson stated flatly. "May I inquire what exactly you're looking for?"

"I'm working on three deaths. All caused by strychnine and all traced back to your chocolate." Derrek said flatly.

"That's impossible!" Lawson said sharply. "I think I need to refer you to our legal department. Please hold." the line went silent and once again the woman's voice began promoting a line of hard candy.

Derrek spent the next thirty minutes being passed around until he finally reached the office of Raymond Leslie, who announced himself as Chief Legal Counsel for the company.

He was brisk as he answered the phone. "I really can't make any comment. If you'll send me the information, I'll see that it's put on the agenda for our next briefing."

"Mr Leslie, I'm dealing with three apparent homicides. Your candy has a direct link to their deaths. Our labs have confirmed that at least sixty percent of your chocolate contains a lethal dose of strychnine." Derrek said sternly.

"I understand. May I give you an address for mailing?" Leslie replied. "I'll look over what you have and get back to you."

Derrek took a deep breath and scribbled the address Leslie gave him. "It will go out overnight mail." Derrek said. "And Mr. Leslie, please don't make me refer this to a higher law enforcement agency."

The phone clicked, and Mr Leslie was gone. Derrek tossed his pencil on the desk and leaned back. The chance of hearing anything from Raymond Leslie and Elegant Design Sweet was remote.

Larry Guthrie gave his wife, Christine, a hug and kiss. The couple had just celebrated their eleventh wedding anniversary and had exchanged Valentine gifts at lunch.

Christine opened the neatly wrapped box of chocolate and opened the lid. "These look so delicious!" she exclaimed as Larry poured two glasses of champagne.

"No need to save them for dinner." Larry said, planting a kiss on her forehead.

"Enjoy them," he added as he picked up his briefcase and headed for the door. "I'll see you at five. Be ready. Dinner reservations are at seven," he added and closed the door.

Christine Guthrie wouldn't make dinner that night. She would be dead on the dining room floor an hour later. It was the fourth body in as many days and the deaths had now spread to the town of Harris some fifty miles away.

Helen and I sat at the breakfast table reading the morning paper. The recall on all boxes of candy from Sandy's Sensational Sweets was on the front page. The newspaper didn't provide any details, just mentioned that you needed to return the boxes to the shop unopened. "What type of individual would do something like that to total strangers?" I asked

"I don't know." Helen replied, "But I'm not convinced that this is about any one person. I think it's about destroying Sandy Jessop."

"Why?" I asked, reaching for the coffeepot to refill our mugs.

"Good question." Helen replied, folding the paper. "But someone obviously hates her enough to do this with no regard for who gets hurt."

I leaned back in my chair and locked my fingers behind my head. "Then where do we start?" I asked the ceiling. "

"I want to talk to Sandy about her life before she moved here and who the man she was with in Stu's that one night. This is personal."

I stood and stretched. "I'll go open the shop if you want to stop by her shop."

"Great!" Helen said, picking up her fanny pack. "Have Hattie put her ear to the ground for gossip and ask Mark to do the same. Someone, somewhere, has a lot of hatred and we need to find them."

Helen found Sandy Jessop sitting behind the counter in her shop. There were a few brownies, a dozen oatmeal cookies, and two cakes in the display case.

"No need to bake," Sandy said as she entered. "There aren't any customers."

"Could you pack up four brownies for me?"

Sandy got to her feet and opened a box. "I've got nothing but time," she said, placing the brownies inside and taping the box closed.

"Someone who you know or have had dealings with really hates you." Helen said, handing money over the counter. Sandy made change and shook her head. "Beats the heck out of me," she said, returning to the stool.

"I'm not trying to pry, but who were you with in Stu's the other night?"

"Oh, him." Sandy said, smiling. "His name is Walter Reynolds. He's from Harris and we went to school together." "Any reason for Walter to have it out for you?" Helen asked.

Sandy shook her head. "No, we just hadn't seen each other in a couple years and wanted to catch up."

"What does Walter do for a living?" Helen asked.

Sandy smiled. "He teaches third grade at Harris Elementary. I'm sorry, but he's as harmless as a blade of grass." She added.

Helen picked up the box. "Sandy, someone really, really hates you. If we're going to find out who is responsible, you're going to have to tell me who in your past has a grudge bad enough to kill for."

Sandy shook her head. "I don't know." She said flatly. "I am really trying to think of someone. I gave the Chief a list of the three people who I had any lasting relationships with back in the city. But outside of that, I honestly don't know."

Helen studied her for a moment. "Try a little harder. We're behind you, but you've got to help us."

Sandy nodded, and Helen made her way back across the street to our shop.

Hattie and Mark had stopped by and I had asked them to put out feelers about who would hate Sandy Jessop enough to run her out of business.

Both of them said they would, but felt it was hopeless Since Sandy wasn't from Heaven. Mark noted there might be many individuals in her past who intended to harm her.

Derrek started running background checks on the three people who had had long-term relationships with Sandy Jessop when she ran her business in New York City. It would take about forty-eight hours to complete them.

In the meantime, there were still over half of the red candy heart boxes out in the public somewhere. The recall notice was in four regional papers, and there was hope that they would either return or dispose of the remaining half of the red candy heart boxes.

The Harris police chief was on the phone to Heaven. Chief Roger Towne had what looked like a murder on his hands. The red heart-shaped candy box found at the scene was a link to Heaven and the candy store.

"Yes, Chief" Derrek said. "We're having our own issue with poison from those boxes. I can be there in an hour." A moment later, he hung up the phone. Another woman was dead after eating candy from the sweet shop. That brought the total to four and Derrek couldn't help but wonder how many more would die before they found the mysterious killer.

He picked up the phone and dialed the number of Sandy Jessop.

"Sensational Sweets," her voice came on the line.

"Sandy? Chief Landly."

"Yes, Chief."

"There's been another incident. This one up in Harris."

There was an audible gasp.

"Do you know a woman named Christine Guthrie?" Derrek asked.

"No, I'm afraid I don't," Sandy replied.

"Okay, just needed to ask. How many boxes have you had returned so far?" Derrek asked

"As of right now, I have thirty-seven. That leaves about forty boxes unaccounted for." Sandy said and took a deep breath. "Is there anything else we can do?" she asked.

"Nothing I know of. Just pray that most people have thrown out those boxes.

The line was silent.

" No one is praying harder than I am," she said and hung up the phone.

"We need to know more about the store that shipped the candy to Sandy." Helen said to the group of us gathered in our back room.

"It's in New York City," Mark said. "Do you think one of us should go there?"

Helen shook her head. "They won't to talk to us. I'm sure Derrek has been in touch with them and if they are anything like most big companies, they will circle the legal wagons."

We all fell silent. "Does Sandy know anyone who works there that would have a grudge against her? "

"She didn't mention it, but we certainly need to find that out," Helen said.

There is someone out there that is an insane killer and doesn't care who dies, or there's someone targeting Sandy and her business.

"Boyfriend?" Hattie asked.

"Good thought. I will check with her later." I said. "There is the man she was seen with at Stu's,"

"Got that one checked out this morning." Helen replied. "He's an elementary school teacher out of Harris."

"This is impossible." Mark said, getting to his feet. "I'm going online and check out this New York City Sweet Company. After all, the poison candy came from there."

We all nodded in agreement. Yet, both Helen and I thought that there had to be someone between the candy company and the shop. A more local connection.

CHAPTER 6

Why was she still there? Why was the shop still open? Surely the deaths had to be linked to her shop and the candy. Surely she had to be suspected by the police. So why was she still open for business?

He paced the floor and opened another bottle of beer. At the time it had all made sense. And it had been expensive to pay off his connection in New York. He had also had to travel out of state to get the quantity of strychnine that was needed. It had cost him a tidy sum of his savings.

He had to cover his tracks and be sure there was no trace of his involvement that the police could discover. The new chief's intelligence made him constantly worried about the possibility of the police discovering him at any moment.

"Stay cool, and calm and don't panic," he told himself out loud. "Don't panic," he repeated as he walked to the front window and looked down at the street. It didn't matter how many people the candy killed. What mattered was that Sandy Jessop paid for what she had done.

Chugging his beer, he focused on the front of the candy store. It had to stop. She had to go, leave the place. She had no right to be there and if poisoning random people with her candy wasn't enough, then he'd have to eliminate her.

The background checks were complete, and none of the three men Sandy had connections to in New York had any connection to Elegant Design Sweets. The victims had no connection to the pastry chef, hedge fund manager, and playboy.

He sent the request for information about Sandy's order to Raymond Leslie via overnight mail, not expecting aid without a court order.

The Harris chief of police had shared all the information he had about the victim, Christine Guthrie. She and her husband Larry had lived in the same middle class neighborhood for ten years.

Larry worked as a loan executive at a local bank for nearly ten years. They had little debt and were not in financial trouble. Neither did the couple have children or any close relatives.

"Clean as a whistle." Derrek said to himself as he reread the information. "Just a chocolate lover," he added.

Hattie tapped on the glass door fifteen minutes before opening. Helen spun the lock and let her inside. "Listen, I did a lot of thinking last night about this thing with Sandy," she said, making her way to the office.

"That location where the sweet shoppe is located has a dark past." She said, sitting down in a chair.

"Don't you remember Helen?" Hattie asked as she accepted a cup of coffee.

"I remember it sat empty for years." Helen said, "but that's the extent of my recollection." Helen said, sitting down.

"Well, it sat empty for a reason." Hattie said. "There was a fire about fifteen years back. The shop used to be a toy train business. A woman, whose name escapes me, apparently somehow set it on fire and her husband died."

Helen knit her brow "Oh, now it's coming back to me." she said "Someone went to jail for arson or assisting in arson."

Hattie raised her eyebrows. "I'll have to do some digging, but this might be a reason to kill."

"I'm confused." I interjected. "Why would a fire, even a murder, have anything to do with Sandy Jessop?"

"I don't know yet," Hattie said. "But there was something screwy about the entire thing. Maybe ask Chief Landly about it?"

Edith Watts liked her job at the sweet shop. She liked the work, and she liked her boss. Now, with all this business about poison, she wondered if she'd even have a job after things settled down.

She made her way to the shop and tapped on the back door. Sandy was always around the kitchen and would open the door if she heard the rap. Edith waited patiently and rapped louder. She wondered if Sandy might be up front with customers. After a few minutes, she pushed her bicycle through the alley and leaned it against the corner of the building.

The lights were on and she could hear the soft music of the local radio station that Sandy always had on as background noise.

Pulling the front door open, she called out, "Miss Jessop? You back there Ms. Jessop?" There was no answer, so Edith made her way around the display counter and through the swinging doors to the back room.

It was then that she screamed and ran.

I was looking out the front window by the cash stand when something caught my eye.

Edith Watts was running between cars across the street from the sweet shop straight toward me.

I had barely got to the front door when she arrived and literally fell into my arms. "She's dead! She's dead! Someone killed Ms. Jessop!" she shouted and collapsed into my arms.

Helen ran as fast as possible across the street and into the sweet shop. Sandy Jessop lay on her back in the middle of the kitchen. The large mixer turning dough slowly. A spatula in one hand and the phone receiver in the other.

Helen knelt beside her and found a weak pulse. Pulling the phone from Sandy's hand, she dialed 911.

Minutes seemed like hours as we waited for the EMTs and police. I sat Edith down in our back office, got her a bottle of water, and asked her for details.

She explained that she just wanted to check her schedule for the coming week and after there was no answer at the back door; she came to the front, entered and found Sandy on the floor.

It was over an hour before Helen returned to the shop with Derrek. He sat with Edith for a few minutes before joining us at the front.

"I'll see that she gets home," he said. "I'm going to start the paperwork, and then I'll be over at the hospital to check on Sandy." A moment later, he was gone.

Helen shook her head. "It's going to be close." She said.

"The EMT said she's had a severe blow to the head and possibly other injuries. Looks like someone came up behind her." She shook her head. "We have to figure this out soon."

Hattie shook her head. "This has gone too far." She said flatly. "Way too far."

Mark sat next to her in a back booth at Stu's. We were waiting for Helen. She had gone to the hospital to check on Sandy. She was going to stop by the police station to ask Derrek to check into the history of the building the sweet shop was in.

It was nearly an hour before she appeared and dropped into the booth beside me. Mark signaled the waitress that we were ready to place our order, and she appeared almost immediately. With dinner ordered and wine poured, it was time for Helen to fill us in on Sandy and her conversation with Derrek.

"Sandy has a very serious skull fracture, and a fractured eye orbit. They have her in intensive care to monitor any brain swelling that might result from the blow. There is bleeding in the brain and they may have to release the pressure if it continues. She hasn't regained consciousness."

Mark shook his head. "Sounds like a very close call," he said. "If Edith hadn't come along, she might have died."

"With the extent of the bleeding, she couldn't have had much time left." Helen said, rubbing her neck to release tension.

Our food arrived, and we worked our appetites as best we could.

On our second glass of wine, Mark asked, "What happened when you spoke to Derrek?"

Helen took a deep swallow of her wine. "He'd like more information if we have it. But he's willing to investigate all leads."

Hattie took a deep breath. "I've been trying to piece together those events. Best I can come up with, it started about twenty years ago. There had been a bank robbery up in Del Mar. The thieves stole an amount of gold bars. Long story short, they have never found the loot. A few months later, a fire gutted the train shop, which was located where the sweet shop is now. They held the wife of the owner responsible, and I believe she served a few years in jail and died there.

"Building got sold and renovated but never had a successful business in it. Mind you, this was about fifteen years ago."

"I can't remember names or the exact timeframe, but it's been empty now for years. The bank owed it and that's who Sandy purchased it from. Hattie sipped her wine. "It may not be relevant, but it aligns with the past problems faced by businesses using that shop."

We all sat in silence for a few minutes, trying to wrap our minds around the history of the building that housed the sweet shop. "You need to tell Derrek all that you remember." Helen told Hattie. "First thing tomorrow. I'll go with you."

Hattie nodded. "No problem. If you think it will help, I'll try to dig up some history on that property." "Right now, anything will help." Helen said as we made our way to our cars.

CHAPTER 7

Hattie sat at the conference room table with Helen and Derrek. Forty-eight hours had passed since Sandy Jessop's attack. She remained in a coma and the doctors were, at best, cautionary, optimistic.

"So tell me what you've discovered." Derrek said.

Hattie cleared her throat and opened the thick photo album scrapbook in front of her.

"This dates back twenty-five years." She said, flipping a few pages. "This is the same building that the sweet shop is in now." She pointed to a photograph.

"Looks different." Derrek remarked, pulling the book closer.

"It is different. This photo is a little over twenty years old. Back then it housed Jefferson Model Trains." she pointed to the sign.

Scott and Ruth Jefferson operated the business. As best as I can piece together, they had been in Heaven for sometime and ran a successful business.

Derrek nodded. "Why would you associate this with what is happening now?" He asked.

"Well, because there was a bank robbery about fifteen years ago up in Del Mar. The thieves stole a fortune in gold bars and vanished. About six months later, the train shop suffered a dangerous fire. They found the body of Scott Jefferson in the rubble. The fire chief back then was suspicious and did an extensive investigation. It was determined that the fire was an act of arson, and Scott Jefferson had been a victim."

Derrek was scribbling notes on a pad and stopped."Was there a conviction in that case?" He asked.

"Yes," Hattie replied. They arrested and convicted Ruth Jefferson, the wife, of arson and insurance fraud. She received a prison sentence, and she died there.

"Interesting. But what does that have to do with now?" Derrek asked.

"Well, the shell of the building sat untouched for a couple of years until the bank foreclosed on the mortgage. After that, they hired a contractor to rehab and rebuild the building. The bank intended to rent out the space as retail and recoup some of their investment."

Derrek nodded and slowly flipped the page in the scrapbook." Looks like there was a lot of damage." He remarked, pointing to a picture of the aftermath.

"Yes, there was a lot of damage and the bank invested a sizeable chunk of money rehabbing it." Hattie said, leaning back in her chair.

"So? They never were successful in renting it?" Derrek asked.

"Correct. They had a few tenets over the years. Shoe store, woman's clothing and such. They all seemed to fail after a few months. For whatever reason, no one stayed long." Hattie took a deep breath and sipped her mug of tea.

"According to some people around here, the building is said to be haunted or cursed, and that's why no one stayed," she added.

"I hardly think that was the case." Derrek replied. "And it was more than a ghost that whacked Sandy on the head," he added.

"Think what you want. That's the history of that building and to me it would seem as if whatever is happening with the poison candy and now the assault is related to its past."

Derrek leaned back in his chair and tapped his pen on the table. "I'll look into it, Hattie." He said. "Mind if I keep this scrapbook?"

"It belongs to the public library. I checked it out last night. So make sure you return it." Hattie said, getting to her feet. "Someone is determined to shut down Sandy Jessop's sweet shop," Hattie said before leaving.

"I hope it's not too late," she added and was gone.

Derrek studied Helen's face for a moment. "Do you think that's what is going on?" he asked.

"I think it's something close." Helen said. "Heaven has a way of hanging onto things, perhaps even ghosts." She said as she pulled the door open.

Derrek sat and flipped through the scrapbook, that covered a period of about twenty years. There were clippings from the bank robbery in Del Mar and even a picture of Ruth Jefferson alongside her obituary. She had died in prison of a heart attack about eighteen months into her three-year sentence.

Whatever secrets the building had housed were buried for a long time.

Why wasn't she dead? How could she have lived after the blows he struck?

He paced back and forth and wondered how to proceed now that Sandy Jessop was still alive.

Perhaps she would still die. Perhaps the blows from the hammer had been enough, but there had been nothing in the paper that seemed to point that direction. The article reported she was in critical condition and the doctors had airlifted her to the trauma unit in Harris.

That presented a challenge. How could he get into that unit and finish her? Should he try? Should he wait? He needed more information. But how?

He pulled open the phone book and found the main number of the hospital and dialed.

The woman who answered didn't seem alarmed that a doctor from Heaven was checking on his patient. The request for information on Sandy Jessop did not bother the nurse at the intensive care unit.

"Yes, doctor, there has been no change. Dr. Phillips has released the pressure on the brain with two burr holes. Her vitals have stabilized and we are hopeful she will stabilize further during the next forty-eight hours. "

"Yes, doctor, the patient is still critical, but stable."

He hung up the receiver and clinched his fists. "Why wasn't she dead?"

It had been easy to open the back door of the sweet shop quietly.

The noise from the commercial mixer had muted any sound from his approach. He knew she hadn't seen him. Her back was toward him when he picked up the heavy hammer and struck the first blow. It had sent her to the floor. Crumpled her like a piece of tissue. The other three blows were easy. So why wasn't she dead?

He picked up his coffee mug, took the last mouthful of the cold liquid in his mouth, and hurled the mug against the wall. It shattered. Shattered just like his life had shattered so many years ago.

Hattie sat with Helen and me in the back office of the shop. She shook her head and picked at the napkin her mug sat on. "I wish there was more." She said finally.

"What more would there be?" I asked. "You gave Derrek all there was. The robbery, the fire, the local history of businesses that failed. What more is there?"

Hattie shook her head. "I just feel that there's something missing." She finished the mug of coffee and stood. "Best be getting back to my shop." She said and headed to the door.

Helen thought for a moment. "You know, I had forgotten most of that entire saga. But now that I think about it, there was an employee, young man." She chewed the end of a pencil.

"He was an odd sort of person, but he worked at the train shop and had some connection to the family."

"So? Probably moved on with his life. It's been a long time." I said.

"You're probably right." Helen said. "Still, something about him wasn't quite right." Her eyes drifted to the shop across the street. "Something isn't right." She added and fell silent.

KATEYAZOWSKI

CHAPTER 8

Derrek had spent the morning doing research into the bank robbery in Del Mar and the arson fire at the train shop.

The bank robbery piqued his interest. An armor car was transporting five million dollars of gold bullion from the First National Bank of Del Mar to the state exchange a hundred miles west. The transfers were routine. First National received gold from the Federal reserve and distributed it to regional centers.

The heist occurred during the transfer from the vault to an armored car. In fact, the car itself was a phony. According to what the federal agency had put together, the thieves hijacked the actual car before it arrived and replaced the guards.

Once at the bank, all they had to do was wait for the bullion to be loaded and drive away. A hunter found the guards bound and gagged about twenty miles from the bank in a wooded area.

It was clever, clean, and almost foolproof. No faces that were remembered, no fingerprints, no trace where they went after driving the car into the woods.

The train shop had been in business for over ten years at the time of the fire. Until then, there was nothing to arouse suspicions that there was a problem with the business or the owners. Scott Jefferson was popular among the business community. The shop's business license showed two employees. A Raymond Hoff who acted as store manager when the Jeffersons weren't around and a Charles Jefferson, who helped his father with the ordering, assembly and display of the merchandise.

Hoff apparently moved to Harris a year after the fire and there was no information on the Jefferson's son after the fire and conviction of his mother. Based on the information, Charles Jefferson believed the court did not treat his mother fairly. He had done a few interviews for the local paper. After Ruth Jefferson died, there was no further mention of Charles Jefferson.

The four businesses that had rented the space after the bank reconstructed the building were also all defunct. Apparently, none could withstand their months in the building financially.

Derrek made note of the names and dates that were available, dropped the scrapbook at the library and returned to the station to piece it all together.

Sally Collins waved a finger at him as he came through the door. "You have a visitor." She whispered.

Sandy was called to the window, leaving Derrek to wonder who was waiting in his private office.

Opening his door, a smile crossed his face. "Well, I'll be!" he exclaimed.

"Didn't think you'd mind if I waited in here," a familiar voice replied and extended a hand.

Ed Hanson, dressed in a dark business suit, shook Derrek's hand vigorously. "Good to see you, my friend," he said, smiling.

"And you as well," Derrek replied, returning the handshake. "What brings you to Heaven again?" he asked.

"Well, to be honest, I got wind of the agency's interest in this poison candy case," he said, as Derrek motioned for him to take a seat.

"It's been nasty." Derrek acknowledged. He added that they're still hoping for the return or disposal of the candy out there.

Ed nodded. "I hope so too. But the interest the agency has is in Sandy Jessop herself."

Derrek arched his eyebrows. "I had her checked, she's clean," he replied.

"I know" Ed said. It's who she is and not her innocence that interested the agency.

"Who she is?" Derrek asked. "She was born and raised in Harris, went to a couple of fine schools. She ran a successful business in New York and now she's here."

"Correct," Ed replied. "Ever hear about a bank robbery up in Del Mar about fifteen years ago?"

"As a matter of fact, I have. Just got the local skinny on that yesterday." He tapped the folder on his desk. "I've been doing a bit of follow up," he added.

"Sandy Jessop's father was the manager of the bank that was robbed." Ed said, leaning forward. "It would seem he was clear of any involvement. But, as the investigation continued to dig into backgrounds, it became apparent that there was possibly a connection to one robber."

"Nothing could be proven, but someone reliably informed me that one man who took part in the actual heist had previously worked as an employee at the bank he managed. About a year after the robbery, the Jessop family suddenly had an influx of cash. Sandy was just collage age, and they sent her off to business school."

"After that, they paid for her culinary school and put up nearly five hundred thousand dollars to help her open the Manhattan store." Ed opened his briefcase and handed Derrek a folder. "It's all there. Parents are dead and there's nothing to show that Sandy ever had any knowledge about their connection to the heist."

"So now she's on some kind of agency watch list?" Derrek asked

"Nope, not at all. But the agency thinks that there is someone in this area that has involvement in that heist. It appears they are targeting her for something they think she knows."

Derrek took a deep breath. "WOW!" he exclaimed. "You know," he said, "they attacked her the day before yesterday and she's in critical condition up in the Harris Trauma Unit."

"I'm aware of that, and I have an agent keeping a close eye on her."

Derrek nodded. "So what's next?" he asked.

Hanson stood and grinned. "Looks like we're working together on a case," he said.

Derrek smiled. "Looks like," he replied.

I went out for deli sandwiches at noon. The shop had been busy and both of us needed food.

As I crossed the street, I noticed the lights were on in the sweet shop. My curiosity peaked. I thought perhaps Edith had opened the shop in Sandy's absence.

The bell on the front door jangled as I opened it. There were no lights on in the front, but the kitchen lights were on and I heard movement. "Hello?? Who's there?" I called, making my way through the swing gate into the back bakery. Three steps inside, someone rushed past me and I went down on my knees. As I recouped my bearings, I saw the legs of a man wearing jeans run through the back door.

"Hey, what the heck are you doing?" I yelled and scrambled after him.

It was no use by the time I made the alley. He was gone, and it was empty. I brushed myself off and made my way back to the sidewalk. Noticed that my left knee appeared to be bloodied, I limped along to the deli and picked up our order.

Twenty minutes later, I limped through the back door of our shop. "I'm back, a wounded warrior!" I called out to Helen.

She appeared in the office doorway. "What the heck happened? Did you fall?" She asked, noticing the wet blood stain on my knee.

"More like pushed." I replied, limping toward her.

"Come sit down." She said. "We have company."

As I got to the office door, shined shoes and a dark suit caught my attention. "Well, I'll be if it isn't Ed Hanson," I exclaimed, as he took my elbow and guided me to the chair.

"At your service, Miss Kathy," he replied. "Now what happened to you?" he asked.

I sat with a thud in the office chair and took a deep breath. "There was someone in the sweet shop, and when I tried to see who, he shoved me down and ran."

"Any idea who?" Ed asked.

I shook my head. "Not a clue."

Helen arrived with the first aid kit and was attempting to roll up my pant leg. "Hold still!" she instructed and proceeded with ointment and band-aid on the scuffed up skin.

"I'll be back." Ed said and walked out the front door just as Hattie walked in.

"What is he doing here?" Hattie asked, making her way to the coffeepot.

"Helping with the investigation into who poisoned these people," Helen replied as I shook down my pant leg and stood up.

Ed returned after finding no trace of who could have been in the sweet shop. "I would suggest that someone get those locks changed immediately." He said.

"I'll take care of it." Helen replied and picked up the phone.

"Well, well, Miss Hattie, you're looking as fit as ever." Ed said as Hattie gave him a hug.

"Any information that you girls dig up I'd appreciated being in the loop." His eyes shifted between the three of us. "I believe that there is a very dangerous person out there and he will not stop soon."

He had to get to the secret spot. He knew the hidden spot was still waiting for him all these years. All the others were gone. Two dead, one is a prison for a different crime. So, he had waited. He had been patient, and he was so close he could almost smell his prize.

Through the years, there had been other problems. Other people had gotten in his way, but every time he'd outsmarted them. He'd gotten rid of them. Now she was here. She was stopping him. She wouldn't go away. Never go away.

She had changed things. She had made the kitchen bigger. The space was all wrong and he no longer knew where the spot was that he needed. He needed time. He needed space. He needed Sandry Jessop gone. Dead. Dead and gone, and he was going to have to do it himself.

He double-checked the duffle bag. He had to look the part. He had purchased green scrubs online. He had the stethoscope and the right shoes.

The bus was on time, and he took a seat at the rear. It was only a forty-five-minute ride to Harris and he wouldn't need much time there. Just long enough to make sure the job was done.

CHAPTER 9

Ed Hanson sat with Derrek at the table in his office. They had the medical reports, autopsy reports, family interviews, and background checks on Sandy Jessop and her New York connections laid out before them.

The two men had been studying them for hours and still nothing connected the crimes with anyone in Heaven, Harris or Del Mar.

"What about this Elegant Design Sweets?" Ed asked.

"New York company. They supplied the hard creams and jelly centers that apparently contained the strychnine." Derrek replied. "I talked to their head attorney, and he basically said he wouldn't supply me with any information but would put the item on his agenda."

Ed arched his eyebrows. "What's the jerk's name?"

"Raymond Leslie," Derrek replied. "He's a big city, big name and not helpful."

"Well, let's see if we can change that." Ed replied with a grin as he picked up the phone.

It took only twenty minutes for the phone to ring with Raymond Leslie at the other end of the connection.

"Agent Hanson," he said in a syrupy voice. "I understand that there is some information you need in connection to that poison case in Heaven."

Ed grinned at Derrek. "That would be correct, sir. Please fax all related documents and conversations about the order to the number I'm going to give you?"

Leslie cleared his throat. "I have that file right here and I'd be happy to share it with the agency."

"That's good because there are four people dead and potentially another forty victims still out there. It just wouldn't look good to be involved in those murders."

"Yes, well, no, we certainly wouldn't want that." Leslie cleared his throat. "If you'll give me that fax number?"

Derrek was grinning ear to ear as Ed recited the number into the phone.

"I'll look forward to that fax in the next few minutes," he said. "And thank you, Mr. Leslie, for your help."

"You're welcome." Came the brisk reply, and the connection was broken.

Ten minutes later, here was a nine-page fax on the table between the two men.

Sandy Jessop had a five-year history with the company.

When she ran her business in New York, she relied on them as a primary chocolate supplier.

She had a credit line of over two thousand dollars and a good payment history.

About a week before she opened the shop in heaven, she placed the last order comprising two hundred and fifty pieces of hard cream centers and jelly centers.

The company had shipped them two day air and billed her for the order. She had paid for it four days later. Derrek rubbed his temples. "I don't see anything that's of any help to us."

Ed studied the shipment page and frowned. He reached across the table and picked up the promotional of the shop's opening.

"Well, I'll be," he said out loud and leaned back in his chair. Will you look at this he said handing the paper to Derrek? "The shipment went to an address in Harris and someone apparently reshipped it here a day later." "

"What?" Derrek exclaimed, snatching the paper from Ed.

"Why would it not come directly to her?" he asked.

"Good question." Ed replied and scribbled down the Harris address.

"Let's go find out who or what lives at 305 Wilson Street in Harris." he said as both men grabbed their jackets.

CHAPTER 10

305 Wilson Street in Harris was on the corner in a rundown neighborhood.

Large shrubbery hid most of the front windows of the house, which set back from the street.

Derrek parked the car on the street. He and Ed made their way to the front door and pushed the bell. The house was quiet, but they could hear footsteps approaching the door.

A small woman appeared in the three-inch space the chain lock allowed.

Ed Hanson smiled, "Good afternoon. My name is Ed Hanson and we're looking for the gentleman of the house."

"He aint here." Came the reply and the door started to swing shut.

Ed shoved his foot in its path. "Mind if I ask you where he is?"

"Don't know. He comes and goes," came the reply.

"And what name is he using?" Ed asked, still wedging his foot in the doorway.

"Ha! What a stupid question! Only name he's got is Ray Hoff. Now get your foot out of the door!" she pushed harder and Ed withdrew his foot.

"Thank you," he said as the door slammed shut.

Back in the car, Derrek scanned his notebook. "Ramond Hoff was the manager of the train shop in Heaven back when it was open." he met Ed's eyes.

"I think we have ourselves a connection." Ed replied and reached for his cell phone. "Let's see what we can come up with on Mr. Hoff,"

A stop at the Harris police station yielded nothing. No one had arrested Raymond Hoff in Harris in the past five years. He had no convictions that came up on a background check and his driver's license only showed the Wilson Street address.

On the drive back to Heaven, the two pondered their next move. There was a connection between the candy shipped from New York and the address in Harris. But the residents of that address had nothing to link them to any criminal activity. It looked like a dead end.

"Okay, we know someone shipped it to the Wilson Street address." My question is, who gave that address to Elegant Design Sweets? "I can't believe Sandy gave it to them."

"I think we need to call Mr. Leslie again." Derrek said.

Raymond Leslie sounded perturbed when he answer the phone. "Yes, Agent Hanson, did you not receive the fax?"

"Yes, Mr Leslie I did. But I have a question that perhaps you can answer."

"If I can," came the reply.

"What address do you have from Sandy's Sensational Sweets?"

"One moment," papers rustled in the background.

"45 Main Street."

"Then can you explain how the shipment went to 305 Wilson Street in Harris?" Ed asked

Silence answered his question.

"I don't know that I can answer that. The only address in the file is for Main Street in Heaven," he took a deep breath. "Let me transfer you to the shipping department," he said. The phone clicked and a buzzing sound could be heard.

"Shipping, this Is Molly," a voice came on the line.

"Hi Molly, my name is Ed Hanson. Perhaps Mr. Leslie explained the situation."

"He said you needed to clarify an address for an active investigation." She replied, "I have the account file here. What do you need?

"Can you verify the shipping address for me?" Ed asked.

"The address on file is 45 Main Street, Heaven… is that right Heaven?" Molly's voice asked.

"That is correct. 45 Main Street is where the last shipment would have gone?"

"Oh, hang on." Papers rattled. "No, there was a change of address over the phone. It went to 305 Wilson Street in Harris." Molly sounded doubtful. "It's strange." She added.

"What is strange?" Ed asked.

"We don't normally change shipping through a phone call." We require it in writing on company letterhead.

The handwritten notation on the shipping invoice makes it impossible to trace the responsible party.

"How many people could have made that notation?" Ed asked.

Molly took a deep breath. "Probably at least fifty."

"Thanks Molly, can you fax that sheet with the handwritten change to me?"

"I sure can," she replied as Ed gave her the number.

The fax arrived within a few minutes but offered little help as to who had changed the address or why.

There was a man seated outside Sandy's door. He had on a dark suit and was scanning a local newspaper. This could poise a challenge to his plans. He kept his hands on the medication cart he had taken from another hall.

One nurse was at the desk, and the second was in one of the care rooms. He scanned the layout and slowly pushed the medication cart forward past Sandy's room. He could see her through the glass window as she lay in bed. A variety of machines seemed to monitor her vitals and there were at least three iv drips hung around her bed.

He turned the cart around and pushed it slowly back down the hall. Just past the bank of elevators, he stopped. He took inventory of the medications on the cart. His eyes fell on a syringe labeled Midazolam. The bright red warning label told him it was dangerous and would stop or slow breathing.

He looked around and decided it was his only option. He carefully slid it into the pants pocket of his scrubs and began slowly down the hall. Halfway there, the man in the dark suit stood and stretched. He glanced at his watch and made his way to the desk, asking the nurse for a phone.

It was the opportunity he needed, and he walked quickly past the desk and into Sandy's room. Glancing out the window, he slipped the needle into one of the IV bags, shoved the plunger, and withdrew the syringe.

Thirty seconds later, he was past the desk and approaching the elevator when the loudspeaker boomed

"CODE BLUE ICU 4! CODE BLUE ICU 4!"

The man smiled and punched the down button. He'd be home in an hour and Sandy Jessop would be gone. In a few days, it would be his again. He smiled.

"DAMN IT" Ed Hanson was gripping the phone receiver so tight his knuckles were white. "HOW THE HELL DID THIS HAPPEN DAVID?"

Derrek sat behind his desk, eyes fixated on Hanson. The phone call had come from Harris a couple of minutes earlier. There had been another attempt on Sandy Jessop's life. This time right under the nose of the protective detail Ed had assigned to watch her.

"It's not acceptable! You get a man over there and damn it, pay attention!" Ed said sternly. "Let me talk to the doctor."

"What's her current condition?" Ed asked and perched on the

corner of Derrek's desk.

"I see. Please do everything you can." he cradled the phone and shook his head.

"Someone got to her," he said, getting to his feet. "Right under our nose and nobody knows how or who or any damn thing."

"How is she?" Derrek asked.

"Hanging on by a thread" Ed shook his head and paced back and forth. "They aren't sure exactly what, but it appears someone injected her with some drug that suppressed her breathing." They have her on a respirator, and have given her medication with the hope she can pull through."

Derrek shook his head, "Someone has a real grudge against that lady." He said and yawned. "How about we get some rest and start again in the morning?"

Ed took a deep breath. "I guess you're right." He picked up his jacket. "Drop me at the hotel?"

"You bet," Derrek said, turning out the lights.

"If anything happens, you call me," he told the dispatcher on his way past the desk. "And, I mean anything."

CHAPTER 11

It was a little after nine in the morning. Light snow drifted down and the temperature was dropping.

Derrek had called us at seven asking if we could meet him and Ed at the sweet shop around nine.

The four of us stood in a line just inside the kitchen door. "What exactly are we looking for?" Helen asked.

"I wish I knew," Ed replied. "Someone is willing to kill over this shop. My assumption is that there must be something here he wants, or needs."

I looked at Helen. "Like gold?" I asked.

"I doubt it, but who knows? Let's just systematically go through the place. If something looks odd, feels odd or doesn't fit, sound off."

We searched for nearly three hours. We touched walls, pipes, counters and Derrek got a ladder and checked the ceiling. It was to no avail. If the killer wanted something that was hidden here, it sure wasn't obvious to any of us.

I called Hattie and Mark to meet us at the diner for brunch with the thought that maybe one of them had come up with something that would help.

We piled into the large corner booth and ordered brunch specials. As the waitress refilled our coffee cups, Mark said. "Ive been searching the web for anything on this Elegant Design Sweets that keeps popping up. I've also talked to some financial friends of mine in the city."

"It wasn't always licensed under that name. That name was filed only twelve years ago by Selaca Corporation, which now is the parent company. In case you're wondering who they are; let me give you a hint. Every time you guys buy a snack cake at a connivence store you're buying something made by Selaca."

"They are a multi-million-dollar conglomerate, and I'm sure they want to cover their backsides in relation to these deaths."

"Who had the company before they got it?" Derek asked.

"Well, hang on tight to your cinnamon roll."

"Our good friends, Scott and Ruth Jefferson. There was a partnership formed to finance both the train shop here and the candy shop in New York." he swallowed a mouthful of coffee. "And both businesses were financed by First National Bank in Del Mar." he smiled. "The very bank that was robbed."

We all gaped. "I mean how?" I stammered.

"And there is more. A few months after the bank robbery, the loan was repaid in full by Scott Jefferson. Plus, a deal was negotiated with Selaca for the sale of the New York candy business."

"So now we have a local connection to New York City, but it sounds as if everyone made out well financially." Derek said.

"Not exactly." Mark replied. "There were recipes for several unique chocolates that were supposed to transfer to Selaca but never did.

The friend I talked to in New York said those recipes are worth well over a million dollars, maybe more. Selaca would love to have them. Maybe enough to kill."

My head was spinning. In fact, it was throbbing from everything that Mark had discovered. Derrek and Ed had grabbed the check and headed back to the station to follow up on the new leads.

"Do you think that this multimillion dollar company would go after someone like Sandy over candy recipes?" Helen asked Mark.

"Maybe not, but there might be someone local who is seeing dollar signs worth killing for." Mark replied, chugging the last of his coffee.

"Any word about how Sandy's doing? Hattie asked.

"Someone got to her last night with some kind of drug." Helen said. "She's on a respirator."

"This is terrible." Hattie said, getting to her feet. "I think I might drive up there today and sit with her."

I smiled. "Do you think she'll know?" I asked.

"She'll know." Hattie replied and was gone.

Helen and I headed home. It was Sunday, and the shop was closed, and we had no plans.

An hour later, we sat at the kitchen table making notes on everything that had happened and the people we knew might be involved. It wasn't a long list, and it seemed to lead nowhere.

We had made a list of all the names of people involved in the incident.

Starting with the known victims: Shelia Whitmore, Becky Wright, Kathleen Johnson and Christine Guthrie

Sandy's past relationships: Peter Robinson, Todd Keller, and Randy Collins. We also added the 3rd grade teacher, Walter Reynolds.

There were the Jeffersons, Scott and Ruth, and their son Charles.

We added in the train shop manager, Raymond Hoff. We also noted that someone had shipped the candy order to his address.

Then we factored in the bank robbery, it too had an odd connection to Sandy. Her father was the bank's manager at the time of the robbery.

The investigation found one of the suspected robbers had previously worked at that bank. That person's name and whereabouts were unknown.

We detailed the missing candy recipes and the fact that the Jeffersons had sold the New York business prior to the fire in Heaven.

Somewhere in this hodgepodge of victims and suspects was the answer to who wanted Sandy Jessop dead.

Mark kept searching to see if the valuable recipes could still be around on the internet but found nothing.

By mid morning on Monday nothing seemed to have changed. Sandy was still in critical condition, and the mystery surrounding the sweet shop remained unsolved.

Ed and Derrek were actively tracking down leads in the Harris area where Christine Guthrie had been killed.

Hattie spent the early mornings at the Heaven Library searching the stacks of scrapbooks and newspapers for any clues we might have missed.

On the conference room table, Derrek had laid out the files on the four victims. The question on his mind was, were they just victims or were they targets?

Shelia Whitmore was the first. She had been a head teller at the village bank for over ten years. Shelia had an engaging personality and knew many people in the village. Was it possible she knew the killer and had contact with him or her through her job?

Becky Wright was young. She worked as a cashier at the local market. She was young, attractive and like to flirt. In fact, she had flirted with more than one married man and had had at least one confrontation with an angry wife. Her personality would seem to make her a target of a good fight with an angry spouse, but not the target of a serial killer who killed at random.

Kathleen Johnson was by far the most innocent of the victims. Her husband had passed several years earlier, and she was a retired schoolteacher with many friends in the area. She kept a tidy house, had a large flower and vegetable garden, sang in the church choir and, as far as we could tell, had absolutely no enemies.

We knew very little about Christine Guthrie, the Harris victim, but she appeared to be a housewife with a husband who loved and supported her. Again, not a person who would be the target of a serial killer.

And so, we diligently completed piece after piece on our list, and as dinnertime approached, we realized we had accounted for everyone except one person. Charles Jefferson, the son of the train shop owners.

Try as we might, there was nothing on him past the age of eighteen. After the fire and the death of his mother, he seemed to disappear. There was no one in town who had employed him, and no one really remembered much about him. Hattie had three newspapers clippings that mentioned him. He had been very vocal after the death of his mother and had accused the court system and people in Heaven of railroading her into prison. The last one, dated nearly eleven years ago, showed his threat to bring a wrongful death lawsuit against the village. It was never filed, and Charles Jefferson seemed to simply disappear.

CHAPTER 12

We were all gathered around the conference table at the Police Station. It held every piece of paper and report that had been collected since the first day of the investigation. Derrek and Ed began investigating family members and co-workers, but they didn't uncover any solid leads.

"So," Ed said, "All the information we have gets us no closer to finding this killer than we were. The victims are random, their families have no connection to each other, and we can't even connect anyone to the sweet shop or its past owners."

"We may have something to work on." Helen said.

"No one has accounted for the son of the train shop owners. His name is Charlie or Charles Jefferson. From what we found in the local papers, he was a furious young man after his mother died in prison. He threatened to sue the village and just about everyone in it." Helen told the group.

Ed turned to Derrek. "Do you know this guy?" he asked.

"Nope, he hasn't been arrested here," he replied. "I would remember." Derrek said.

Ed tapped the end of his pencil on the table. "Anyone here know this guy?" he asked.

"Hattie only remembers the threats he made about suing the village." Helen said. "But she has no memory of where he went or even what he looks like."

A tap came on the door and Sally Collins popped her head in. "Sorry Chief, but there's a gentleman here that says you want to see him?"

"Who?" Derrek asked, getting to his feet.

"A Raymond Hoff" Sally replied.

We all exchanged a quick look, and Derrek motioned to Ed. "My office." He said to Sally.

Raymond Hoff was a thin man in his early seventies. He wore a shirt that was at least one size too big and jeans. He sat erect on the edge of the chair in front of Derrek's desk.

"Mr. Hoff. Thanks for coming in." Derrek said, extending a hand.

"Welcome." Hoff replied, shifting his eyes to Ed.

"This is Special Agent Ed Hanson." Derrek said as a way of introduction. "He's assisting us in our investigation."

Ed extended a hand, which Hoff shook before returning his eyes to Derrek. "The woman said you were at the house the other day," he said.

" Sorry I missed you, been out looking for work," he added.

"I understand." Derrek said, dropping into his chair. "We have some questions about a box of chocolate that was delivered to your address."

Hoff knit his brow. "Chocolates?" he asked. "Must be some mistake. I didn't order any chocolates. Got no money for that stuff."

"How is that possible?" Ed asked. "You don't know that a box has been delivered?"

Hoff shook his head. "Look, I aint been home much for the past month. A box could sit on that front step for days if the woman didn't come out that door."

"I came here to help, if I can. But I don't know nothing about a delivery of chocolate." he shook his head. "Wish I could help." He added.

"Is that Mrs. Hoff that we spoke with?" Ed asked.

"The one and only." Hoff said and chuckled. "She aint much but I care for her and she's a good cook." he smiled. "We's been together for over ten years." he added.

"Can we call her and ask if she saw a box on the steps?" Derrek asked.

Hoff shook his head. "Got no phone." Hoff said. "Can't afford one."

Derrek nodded. "Ok, let's talk about when you were here in Heaven at the Train shop."

"Oh,now, there's some history." Hoff said. "Long time ago."

"Tell us about the Jeffersons," Ed prompted.

Hoff shrugged. "Not much to tell. The Mrs was as odd as a three-dollar bill. She was good with the customers." He added.

"And Scott?" Derrek asked.

"He was an okay boss. But sneaky. Always trying to make a fast buck," he shook his head. "He'd try anything to get money. And the boy, Charlie, now there's a mental case for you."

"You wouldn't know where we might find Charlie?" Ed asked.

Hoff shook his head. "With his money, he could be on one of those islands," he said. "Don't reckon I'd have any idea. He's a strange one."

"What money are you talking about?" Derrek asked.

Hoff studied the two men for several minutes. "Look, I only know what I was told." He said.

"So this ain't on me, ain't on me at all."

"Okay, but what aint on you?" Derrek asked.

Hoff took a deep breath. "Mind you, I don't know this as a fact. It's only what I picked up when I was working. Maybe listening when I shouldn't have." he looked back and forth between the two men. "So I don't know if it was talk to truth, understand?"

"Understood," Ed said

"Well, what I heard is that the boy and Scott were into a robbery up in Del Mar with a couple of other men. They got a huge haul of gold and brought it back to Heaven. That's why the place burnt, you know. Mrs.wanted to liquidate that bullion but Scott was all about waiting till the heat died down." he shifted his weight in the chair.

"That's why she killed him." He said bluntly. "She and that boy of hers. Knocked him out and set the fire. That woman deserved everything she got and more. The boy was only sixteen, so he wasn't even a suspect." he looked back and forth between Ed and Derrek.

"He should have been. I think the boy was born to kill. Yes sir, born to kill." Hoff nodded and went silent.

"After the fire there was a trial and Mrs.Jefferson went to prison. Do you know what happened to Charlie? Ed asked.

"We offered to take the kid in. Actually moved his stuff into the spare room. I think he spent one night and ran off. I've no clue where he went. Never saw him afterward." Hoff shook his head.

"Far as I know he aint got no relations around here. I figure he got himself a room somewhere and who knows from there? Surprised aint in jail somewhere." Hoff shook his head.

Derrek and Ed exchanged glances. "We appreciate you coming in." Derrek said.

Hoff got to his feet. "Aint no bother. I've never been wanted by the law. Don't plan to start now." he nodded to both men and made for the door.

What do you think?" Derrek asked Ed.

"I think we need to find Charlie Jefferson and figure out what's in that building that he's trying so hard to protect." Ed replied.

Why wasn't there a death announcement? Why wasn't something in the paper? Surely that drug was enough to do the job. Stop her breathing, cause her heart to stop. It had been two days and still nothing to indicate he had been successful.

He paced the floor and looked out the window. All those people, shopping and walking back and forth.

All those people, some of whom had helped kill his mother. There was nothing he could do to make them pay for what they had done to his family. The law wouldn't help. He had tried and failed. They liked candy. And one by one, he would have his revenge.

She didn't even remember. Didn't even care. She had sat next to him in school. He'd registered at the high school in Harris. Even found himself a cheap room. And she was there. Every day, she was there.

He knew her father was the bank manager. He knew her father was a person who had to have known about the robbery plans. He knew a former employee had intimidated her father to keep his mouth shut.

It was her fault that his father never got to enjoy the money. Her fault that his mother was dead. Died in a cage like a rat. It was all her fault.

CHAPTER 13

Investigator Phil Rogers retired from the Del Mar police department several years ago. During his twenty plus year career, he'd handled a lot of cases. He prided himself on the fact he had solved most of them. But there was one case that had eluded his resolution.

The gold robbery of the First National Bank had been the largest in the state's history. Estimates were that the thieves had made off with well over thirty million dollars in gold bullion. No one had ever found the stolen gold bullion, and authorities had never caught the thieves.

 The Del Mar police chief had called to ask if Rogers would meet with the Heaven Chief of Police and Special Agent Ed Hanson regarding the robbery. Now he wondered exactly what the people from Heaven had to offer.

He sat in the River House Restaurant looking out over the valley and wondering if maybe there had been a development that would solve his one open investigation.. The waitress refilled his coffee, and he noticed a police cruiser pulling into the lot. His company from Heaven had arrived.

Derrek noted that Phil Rogers was tall and thin with thick silver gray hair and an oversized moustache.

"Thank you so much for meeting with us," Derrek said, extending a hand.

"This is Special Agent Ed Hanson, who is assisting with the investigation."

The men shook hands and ordered coffee. The restaurant was busy, but Rogers had selected a booth at the rear and it was reasonably private.

"I understand from the Chief that you seem to have a connection to the bank robbery here?" Rogers asked.

"We do." Derrek explained.

Ed related the case they were working on and how the robbery somehow seemed to fit in.

"Well, I worked that case for over ten years. Made no actual progress. It was a damn clever heist." Rogers said, leaning back in his seat.

"They hijacked an armor car out of Stevens. I found no link between the guards in the actual car and anyone at the bank here. It seems the robbers faked an accident that blocked the road. The car stopped, and they somehow tricked one guard into getting out.

We found tear gas in the abandoned car and the guards vaguely remembered passing out. A passerby found them several hours later, gagged and tied to trees.

"So, the robbers put on their uniforms, and when they got to the bank, simply went about loading the gold and driving away." he shook his head. "We had practically nothing to go on." he shook his head.

"We're interested in the suspicion that surrounded the bank

manager." Derrek said.

"Frank Jessop." Rogers said, nodding his head. "He had been manager there for several years. Didn't have a record and seemed responsible."

"Yet he was a suspect for a while?" Derrek asked.

"No more that the rest of the employees." Rogers sipped coffee. "He had a relationship with a teller who had been fired a few weeks earlier." A man by the name of Ron Holmes. They were golf buddies and Holmes spent some time with the Jessop family. Picnics and such."

Ed scribbled on his notepad. "Jessop fired him?" he asked.

"No, that dismissal came down from the head office. Holmes had lied on his application and that was grounds for termination. Jessop had nothing to do with the termination. He wasn't happy about it and voiced his opinion to the head office."

"Why was Holmes a suspect?" Derrek asked.

Rogers shook his head. "He mouthed off when the termination came down. Said he's get even."

"And did they clear him?" Derrek asked..

"Yes, beyond doubt."

"Tell us about Jessop." Ed said. "We have a situation with his daughter, Sandy." he added.

"As far as I was concerned, I cleared Frank Jessop, but some people associated with the bank made life miserable for him.He hung on for a few months but ultimately quit." Rogers finished his coffee and leaned back in his seat. "I think he was a good man," he added.

"What about the chunk of money he seemed to have about a year later?" Derrek asked.

"I'm aware of that and checked it out throughly." Rogers said. "It was a combination of severance pay and the liquidation of some stocks the family had. I believe that the daughter Sandra was about to apply for collage."

"So as far as your investigation Jessop was clean?"

"Clean." Rogers replied. "They left Del Mar and moved to Harris, I think."

"Your thoughts on the robbery?" Ed asked.

"Brilliant" Rogers said. "Absolutely brilliant. It was four men and millions of dollars' worth of gold. I suppose they are all basking in the sunshine on a beach somewhere."

"No one comes to mind as a suspect?" Ed asked.

Rogers shook his head. "I brought my file," he said. "Made copies of everything when I retired. This case has always stuck in my craw." He laid a large folder on the table.

"Here it is, you're welcome to it. I'd like it back but by all means, if it can help your case," he gestured with his hand. "You're more than welcome to it."

The file was massive. "We appreciate it, and I'll make sure it gets returned." Derrek said.

"Ive got one more question." Ed said, standing.

"Does the name Charlie or Charles Jefferson mean anything to you?"

Rogers thought for a moment and shook his head. "Afraid not," he said.

Ed nodded. "We appreciate your time," he added, and they turned to leave.

The massive file would need to be combed page by page. It was a daunting task, but if it provided a lead into what was happening in Heaven, they were more than willing to do it.

"What do say we stop by and see Hoff's wife on the way home?" Ed asked.

"Great minds think alike." Derrek replied

A half hour later, they rang the doorbell at 305 Wilson Street. A moment later, the door opened and Ray Hoff smiled and motioned them inside.

"You want to talk to the Mrs? "He asked.

"Just a quick question." Derrek said.

"Louise, the cops from Heaven are here. Want to ask you a question." Hoff yelled into a back room.

A moment later the woman who had answered the door appeared. She nodded "Hello again." she said.

"We're sorry to disturb you but we have a question." Derrek said.

"Okay." Louise Hoff said sitting on the arm of a sofa.

"Did you notice a box that had been delivered and maybe sat on your step?"

"Man came and got it." she said nodding her head. "Truck dropped it off, but I thought they maybe left it at the wrong house. Happens all the time." she She said nodding.

"Looked out later that afternoon and it was gone so I paid it no nevermind." She added.

"And you didn't see who picked it up?" Ed asked.

"No sir. Spend most of my time in the kitchen." She added.

"Well, thanks a lot." Derrek said and,they turned towards the door.

"Traffic camera at the light"Hoff said suddenly. "Might have caught someone?" he added.

"Thanks, we'll check." Ed said as they opened the door to leave.

On the way back to Heaven,Ed called the Harris public works department. The camera hadn't worked in several weeks. There was no video captured any time near the chocolate delivery. It was a dead end.

He decided to place another call to the Harris Trama Unit. After all tall, had answered his questions before, he had nothing to loose.

"I'm sorry Doctor, I'll have to refer you to the administrator, the woman's voice said calmly.

"Just to check on my patient?" he asked.

"Yes, I'm sorry but you'll have to talk to Doctor Reynolds, the attending physician.Shall I transfer you?

"Yes." he said and when the line buzzebuzzed,he hung up.

So Sandy Jessup was still alive. Somehow, had managed to save her miserable life. He'd have to find another way. But it would take more planning this time. It would take more cunning to get past the new protocals. He needed to think. He needed to plan. He decided to make a pot of coffee and write. It always helped when he wrote things down.

CHAPTER 14

Hattie was sitting in a chair at the Heaven Chronical newspaper morgue. She was going through papers from nearly sixteen years earlier. Her search was for two things. The Train Shop fire and the Del Mar Bank Robbery.

The paper had covered the armored car heist in Del Mar for three editions. All front-page articles detailing how the robbery had been accomplished.

A month later, the Train Shop fire had warranted front page coverage. There were pictures of the fire and of Scott and Ruth Jefferson.

She moved on through the editions until she found the court proceedings for Ruth Jefferson. A picture of Ruth was center page of the evening addition with the headline CONVICTED.

A month later, she found the primary target she had been searching for. A picture of Charlie Jefferson. This time the headline read "SON TO SUE VILLAGE OVER TRAIN SHOP FIRE."

Picking up the stack of papers, she made her way to the desk and had copies made of all the relevant articles before heading to our shop.

"Here's all I could find about the robbery up in Del Mar and the fire at the Train shop." She announced, dropping the newspaper copies on our desk.

I sorted through the stack until I found the article that displayed pictures of the fire and there he was, a younger Charlie Jefferson. I tried to age his boyish face by fifteen yyears, but still didn't recognize him.

Ed had laid out all the documents given to them by Phil Rogers. "The man was a meticulous iinvestigator he said as he finished. "I doubt he missed a piece of lint."

Derrek sat down and picked up the first report Rogers had filed after the robbery. "Four men, all Caucasian. No notation on facial hair or hair color. All in uniform. Average build, average complexion average weight." he looked up at Ed "A very average group of guys, mascurading as armor car guards drive off into the sunset with over four million in gold bullion and no one notices anything about them." He shook his head. "Brilliant is an understatement." He added.

Ed was scanning a statement given by a bank guard who delivered the bullion on the loading dock. "Roger Miles was one of two bank guards that brought the gold out to the loading dock. There were four wagons of bullion,each carying over two million dollars ' worth. He noted that one guard stayed to the front of the car and accepted the carts from the other guards. Protocol kept the driver in the cab."

Ed sat down and read aloud. "The front guard seemed younger than the rest. Now that I think about it, he seemed to still be suffering from acne."

Derrek took the statement and reread it. "Could be Charlie Jeffereson." he said "But there must be thousands of young men that have acne scars well into their twenties."

Ed nodded. " I suppose, he said reading another statement. "They are all over the place. You know how bad eye witness statements can be. We have four bank guards and they all see different things. Average height, shorter than average, taller than average. Young, old, fat, skinny." he dropped the paper on the table. "Rogers did everything he could come up with to solve this and came up empty," he added.

A knock came on the conference room door and Hattie poked her head in." I think I have something of interest." she said.

"Come in Hattie." Derrek waved his hand. "We're just going over the investigator's reports. What did you find?"

Hattie laid the copy of the newspaper on the table."That's a picture of Charlie Jefferson fifteen years ago." she said, pointing to the largest photo on the page.

Derrek picked up the paper and studied the photo. "Seems familiar, but honestly I can't say I've seen him around, he said.

"Kathy says that he could be the person who knocked her down in the sweet shop. She's not ccertain, but it could be, Hattie said.

Ed raised an eyebrow. "Then he has to be here in town. But where?"

Clint Howard was worried. He had stolen the strychnine from the chemical company he worked for. If he were to be found out, it would cost him his job.

He had also agreed to pick up the delivery of chocolates at the Wilson street address. He had injected them in his garage while his wife made dinner one night. Then disposed of the remaining liquid poison in a nearby dumpster.

It had cost him to reship the box and although he was promised part of the payoff, but he hadn't heard from the man in Heaven.

He sat on the sofa and pondered where his father had hidden his share of the gold. Herman Howard had never revealed how the take from the robbery had been split or where it was hidden. He believed that the Heaven connection had information that would reveal the location. The man had gone silent. And that forced Clint Howard to wait in silence.

He remembered his dad and how he had remained mum about the gold for many years. He never even knew the names of the other men involved until he had discovered a stack of letters exchanged between them. Two were dead now, and the remaining one had dropped off the map. Perhaps he knew where the loot had been hidden, but Clint's best efforts to find him had failed.

So, now he sat in his house in Del Mar and waited. Hoping that the promises that were made would be fulfilled.

Derrek and Ed were going page by page through the file Rogers had given them. The investigation was incredible over 200 interviews. Over a hundred photos, and it was obvious that Rogers had spent the bulk of his time tracking down leads.

Nothing linked what was happening now to the robbery. There was nothing pointing to anyone in Heaven as having involvement as the men read report after report, hope dimmed even further that the Del Mar bank heist had any connection to the poison candy and Sandy Jessop.

"Other than the fact that her father was bank manager, I don't see any link to Sandy." Ed said, leaning back in his chair and stretching. "We may be headed down the wrong path," he added.

Derrek shook his head. "Then where do we go?" He asked. "We've searched the building for clues and found nothing. We've looked at her past relationships, investigated the company that made the candy. And all we know is that someone diverted the box to Harris, and that someone picked it up." he got to his feet and stretched.

Ed took a deep breath and pulled the next stack of reports over in front of him. "Let's keep going," he said and started reading.

I kept looking at the shop across the street and pondering why Sandy had been attacked and why someone had pushed me down and ran. There had to be something there. A connection, a clue, a hint. Something. Helen was standing behind me at the cash stand. Her gaze fixed on the sweet shop as well.

"You're thinking there has to be something there." She said, as if reading my mind.

"Why else would someone attack Sandy and come back? Edith and I both saw a man running. Whoever that is has the secret to this entire case." I said.

"You want to go look again?" Helen asked, holding up the keys to the new locks.

I smiled. "You read my mind."

At lunch time we locked up the shop and headed across the street. Unlocking the front door and turning on the lights, a chill crept up my spine. Somehow, the shop was eerie and quiet. We turned on the lights and glanced around the kitchen.

Everything seemed frozen in time. The dough in the mixer was green molded, the cream on the counter had soured. Flour and sugar sat open where Sandy had been using them.

There was evidence of the EMTs as they had left gauze and tape pieces on the floor.

"Where do we start?" I asked Helen.

"Well, Sandy enlarged this room. The area was too small for her kitchen. So there has to be some indication of where she took out the wall." Helen said, walking further into the room. The flooring was new, as was the paint on the walls. There was the new walk in cooler that sat at the back of the room . Obviously installed by Sandy.

I walked over to the door and pulled it open. It was lined with shelving, some occupied with stale baked goods and half finished chocolate candies. "If this is new, then maybe what we're looking for is underneath it." I said, shutting the door and rubbing my arms from the cold.

"Maybe." Helen said, studying the floor by the door. "Or maybe not." She added, picking up a screwdriver from the counter.

"Look at this little mound," she said, pointing.

I followed her gaze and noted the mound of concrete just past the front corner of the cooler. "That's odd." I said.

Helen dropped to her knees and began using the screwdriver to chip away at the cement. Little pieces flew in every direction for several minutes until the driver hit an open area. Helen looked up at me and smiled.

I grabbed a knife and started chipping off pieces of cement. Soon we had a good size hole that revealed a pocket between the subfloor and the top of the mound.

Helen got to her feet and rummaged in the store office for a flashlight. She found a small pocket light and returned to the hole..

The light flashed across something metal and Helen gasp. Slowly, she reached her hand in and pulled out what looked like a brass jar.

"Oh, my goodness!" she exclaimed and turned the jar around in her hand.

"Is that what I think it is?" I asked and heard my voice shake.

"It's an urn, and the name on it is Ruth Alice Jefferson." Helen said. "This is the cremains of Mrs Jefferson. Someone hid it here and it may explain a lot." Helen got to her feet.

"Go get a large bakery bag. We need to take this to Derrek right away."

The urn sat in the center of Derrek's desk and all of us could do nothing but stare at it. Derrek finally took a deep breath and looked at us.

"Where again did you find this?" he asked.

Helen explained once again where it had been hidden and why we had gone back to the shop to look for clues.

"I've seen a lot of weird things in my career." Ed said but this has to top the list. "Obviously, son Charlie had to have hidden it there. But why?" he asked.

Derrek slid the urn across his desk and turned it slowly. It sparkled in the filtered sunlight from the window.

"What would you say a cremation urn would be made from?" he asked the group.

We shrugged and, I said, "Brass maybe?"

Derrek nodded and opened his desk drawer. He pulled out a pocket knife and carefully scratched the bottom lip of the urn. Flakes of gold metal landed on his desk blotter and glittered.

"Well, I'm willing to bet this urn is pure gold, he said, grinning.

We all looked at each other. A low whistle escaped Ed Hanson's lips. " Holy Mother of God." he said shaking his head. "Charlie had someone fashion an urn out of the gold his father got from the robbery. Then hid the urn in the rubble of the Train shop."

We all looked from him to the urn and back. "There has to be more."Helen said.

"And it has to be there somewhere." Derrek added. "This explains why Sandy was attacked. It also explains you being shoved down and Edith seeing a man run through the back alley."

"Visiting hours." Ed added. "Charlie is somewhere around here and he still visits his mother's makeshift grave.

We all stared at the urn and sat in silence for several minutes.

"We have to find him." Derrek said "We have to find him now, before he kills again."

The plan was to set a trap for Charlie in the sweet shop. A carelessly back door left unlocked under the watchful eye of Derrek and Ed.

Kathy and I would make an obvious entry into the shop via the front door. We'd turn on lights and perhaps do a little cleaning. It was to be a visible type of work around the front counter.

Hopefully, Charlie Jefferson would see the activity and make an attempt to enter the shop after we left.

It didn't work. Not on day one and not on day three. Derrek had waited patiently every night in our shop while Ed had located himself behind the shop, hidden by the dumpster. But, Charlie didn't come, no one came and on day four the plan was abandoned. It was obvious that Charlie Jefferson either wasn't in Heaven or had somehow discovered the plan.

CHAPTER 15

He took a bus to Harris after packing his gear and preparing for what had to be done. He had spent hours detailing his situation and outlining the available options. The shop would be there after he returned. He could always attend to the shop at a later date but Sandy Jessop had to be disposed of and the sooner the better.

This time he would be prepared for the man watching her room and he'd be prepared with a syringe loaded with a poison he knew would kill. With her gone the shop would close, and he would be at peace again. No one would stop him now.

The bus stopped in front of the Starlight Motel and he rented a room for three nights paying cash. the trauma center was a short bus ride away and his plan would be easy to exicute. It was almost nine that evening when he placed a call to Clint Howard. The two would meet for breakfast the next morning. He had a sizable amount of cash for Clint and was confident that Howard would be more than helpful.

Ed sat at the conference room table, the investigation papers spread out around him. It was after midnight and the station was quiet. He'd made a pot of coffee an hour earlier and visited the vending machine for chips and a candy bar.

He was reading the fiftfifteen-year-old report on the Train Shop fire. The fire started in the back workshop at about two in the morning of August twenty first. It had been six months and three days since the Del Mar bank heist.

The blaze was reported by a passerby who had just left the local bar. The fire department responded within minutes and found the building completely engaged. There was nothing to do but try to contain the fire and salvage what they could.

The next day they found a badly burned body in the rubble and further investigation found that gasoline had been used to start the fire. It was ruled arson and two people came forward to report that they had seen Ruth Jefferson in the building just minutes before the fire.

The case seemed entirely circumstancial but the investigation was quite complete. Gasoline was found throughout the building and the traces led to the back door. Ruth Jefferson had purchased a gallon of gasoline at the local station only three days before. It seemed like an open and shut case.

She had filed an insurance claim before the ashes were cold and had the claim been paid, it was worth over a million dollars.

Ruth Jefferson had been convicted of both arson and insurance fraud. Her three-year sentence would end in her death from a heart attack eighteen months later.

He read the local paper's coverage of the angry teenager Charlie Jefferson threatening to sue the village and the fire investigators for thousands of dollars. The case was never filed, and Charlie disappeared from the headlines. At age sixteen, he was considered old enough to be on his own and apparently was quickly forgotton.

It was the autopsy report of what had been presumed to be Scott Jefferson that troubled Ed. Even allowing for the damage done by the fire, remains found didn't seem to match the physical description of Jefferson on his driver's license.

Ed read and reread the report. Something was wrong and, it had been wrong for the past fifteen years.

Proving his suspicions wouldn't be easy, but with a bit of luck and the help of Derrek he might be able to solve the bank robbery, the train shop fire and the poison candy all at one time.

At four thirty, he woke Derrek and went over his suspicions. At five thirty he called the agent assigned to Sandy and explained what needed to be done.

Derrek was reading the reports laid out by Ed at seven thirty. He took a deep breath and leaned back in his chair. "You do know that what you're thinking is going to ignite a fire storm?

"I know. But I think we can not only solve the bank robbery, but the mystery of the train shop at the same time." Ed leaned back in his chair. "All I need to do is make one final phone call." he added.

"If this doesn't work?" Derrek asked.

"I'll take the heat." Ed replied. "It all fits, it all makes sense when you link the two things together." he said getting to his feet. Scott Jefferson and Charlie were both in on that bank heist. There is at least one more person out there that was involved. Could be two." he picked up the last potato chip from the table.

"But one or two, you can bet they are going to have to resolve this soon, starting with Sandy's death."

"So you think her death is the key." Derrek said getting to his feet. "If that's the case it's going to require perfect timing."

Ed took a deep breath. "I know. I know." he replied.

It was settled. Clint Howard was sitting in a back booth at the restaurant. The two had never met so he was constantly watching the front door. When the man entered and made a straight line for his table Clint swallowed hard. This was not the person who he thought he'd be meeting.

"Morning." the man said sliding into the boot opposite Clint.

"Morning." Clint replied hearing his voice squeak. "Nice to finally meet." he added.

Over the next hour, the man laid out his plan to get to Sandy Jessop at the trauma center. Howard was to enter, go to the fourth floor where the ICU was located, and double over with what would look like a heart attack. In the confusion he would make his way down the hall to Sandy's room, inject the poison and leave.

Howard would make a fast recovery and the two would meet at the bus stop down the street. Sandy would be dead and Howard would finally collect on what had been stolen some fifteen years earlier. Maybe he wouldn't get all the money today, but he'd get enough to be comfortable with.

As they left the restaurant together, an unmarked police car sat across the street. The driver, a detective with the Harris police, keyed his microphone.

" One Mary Delta to base.

"One Mary Delta go"

"Subjects are just leaving the restaurant and heading for the bus stop. Advise Agent Hanson that the person with Howard is not Charles Jefferson. Repeat, it is not Charles Jefferson."

The phone on Derrek's desk jingled. Sally Collins was on the line and had a phone call for Ed.

"Hanson." he said into the receiver

"Be advised that we've made visual sightings of the subjects. They just left the restaurant, heading for the bus stop. Agent advises that the subject is not, repeat is not Charles Jefferson."

"Thanks, we're on our way." Ed replied.

He looked at Derrek "The man meeting Howard isn't Charlie," he said.

Derrek frowned "Then who?" he asked

"Let's get to Harris and find out." Ed replied, picking up his jacket.

The main floor of the trauma center was busy. Clint had to wind his way between patients and visitors to reach the elevator. Behind Clint, wearing scrubs was his partner. They rode in silence to the fourth floor and once off the elevator Clint started down the hall toward the ICU unit. Half way down the hall he cried out, grabbed his chest and fell to the floor.

Immediately he was surrounded by nurses and doctors. The man in the scrubs continued down the hallway into the ICU unit.

The man stationed outside Sandy's room was now on his feet watching the activity down the hall intently. Two steps and he was past him, heading into Sandy's room. She lay motionless on the bed with machines clicking and humming all around her.

He slowly removed the syringe from his pocket and reached for an IV port.

"You move and you're dead." a man's voice said behind him. "DROP

IT!"

The man froze. The syringe hit the floor as it slid from his hand. Immedately he was in handcuffs and ushered out of the room. Down the hall Clint was on his feet surrounded by two armed officers.

His plan, his carefully thought out plan had failed, and his brain raced to develop some sort of explanation.

Ed stared through the one way glass at the Harris police station. Beside him Derrek watched the man who was handcuffed to the interview table.

"When did you figure this out? He asked Ed.

"It was the only thing that made sense." Ed said taking a deep breath. "It was the incident report from the Heaven fire department." he added.

"Did you call Rogers?" Derrek asked.

"Yes, he did" a voice said.

They both turned to see Phil Rogers standing behind them. The three men shook hands and Rogers stared through the window at the man who had been a ghost for over fifteen years.

"Unbelieveable, Rogers said. "After all these years." he added.

"We also think we've located at least some of the gold." Derrek remarked. "And you won't believe where." Ed replied.

The handcuffed man stared up into the face of Phil Rogers. The two had never actually met but, somehow, the face was familiar.

"Hello Scott." Rogers said. "Welcome back to the living."

Scott Jefferson swallowed hard. "How did you figure it out?" he asked, looking from Rogers to Ed to Derrek.

"Agent Hanson, put it all together." Rogers said, pulling out a chair.

Jefferson glanced between Ed and Derrek. "I recognize you he said nodding in Derrek's direction. Chief Derrek Landly of the Heaven Police Department." he said, grinning.

Derrek nodded and sat down next to Rogers.

"And you must be Agent Ed Hanson." Jefferson said. "You're a smart fellow. My congratulations."

"You're not so dumb yourself." Ed said, pulling the third chair from the table.

Scott Jefferson nodded. "Thank you." He said. "I suppose you have questions? He asked.

"You have the right to an attorney." Ed replied.

Jefferson shook his head. "Naw, makes no nevermind. I'll tell you what you want to know. I'm caught aint no attorney going to change that."

Phil Rogers leaned forward. "Will you tell me about the bank robbery in Del Mar?" he asked.

Scott Jefferson leaned back in his chair and studied the fly buzzing around the light on the ceiling. He took a deep breath and leaned forward, and studied Rogers for a moment.

"Okay, why not?" he folded his fingers together and for a moment stared off into space.

"There were four of us. Herman Howard, Maynard Perkins, myself and Charlie." he nodded. "Charlie was only sixteen, but he thought of himself as a big man back then." A smile crossed his lips.

"We got the idea from Perkins. He lived up in Del Mar and banked at First National. He cased the place for weeks before we pulled the heist."

I had dealings with him on the side. He had connections to some pot dealers, and I bought weed from him several times. In fact, that's how I met Clint's dad, Herman."he took a deep breath.

Scott Jefferson turned to face Phil Rogers. "You were close." He said, "You actually questioned Maynard a couple of times."

Rogers nodded. "I remember."

Jefferson nodded. "Well, old Maynard was scared. He kept coming down to Heaven and talking about you. Talking about turning himself in." he shook his head. "Ol Ruthie figured he was about to confess and turn us all in. So, one night when he was down in Heaven, she took a hammer to his head and killed him."

Ed and I exchanged glances. "So it was his body, the fire department found in the Train Shop?" he asked.

Jefferson nodded. "Well, we had to do something. So we decided on the fire. You all know the rest of that story."

"And you went into hiding and let her take the rap?" Derrek asked.

Jefferson shrugged. "We figured she'd get off and if everyone thought it was me in the fire, there would be no suspicion about the robbery."

"Charlie knew this?" Ed asked. "This sixteen-year-old kid knew you let his mother take an arson charge?"

"Course he knew. After all, it was her that whacked the guy with the hammer. Arson was better than murder." Jefferson smiled. "He was angry about things, but a little anger is good for a boy."

Rogers took a deep breath. What happened to Howard?" he asked.

Jefferson smiled. "Ol Herman had himself a heart attack about ten years back. And died."

"That's how you know his son, Clint?" Ed asked and Jefferson nodded. "That's how." he said.

"Tell me why you hate Sandy Jessop." Derrek asked. "She had no involvement with the heist."

Jefferson laughed. No, she didn't, but we always thought that her daddy knew about Perkins. His wife was a teller at the bank. Maynard was sure that he knew about the connection." he swallowed and continued. "You interviewed the Perkins woman three times and each time she'd go home and tell Maynard that you were closing in."

"I still don't see the connection to Sandy." Derrek said. "She was a young girl.What could she have possibly known that would connect you to the robbery?

"She heard a conversation. She heard Beth Perkins on the phone talking about the robbery. Talking about how scared she was for her husband, Maynard. She could have put it together any minute. You know she spent time in the bank that summer. Her daddy wanted her to intern there. She could have remembered any minute." Jeffersons face went hard and cold. "Bitch needs to die," he added and his hands closed to fists.

Derrek shook his head. It was the reasoning of an insane person. Sandy Jessop was seventeen when the bank was robbed. The odds fifteen years later of her making any connection were remote at best.

"Where's the gold Scott?" Rogers asked.

Jefferson leaned back in his chair and drew a deep breath. "People been walking on it for years," he said laughing. "Been walking on most of it for years," he added, sitting up straight in the chair.

"Don't know what Maynard did with his cut. But Herman was so scared he'd be found out that he left his cut with me. We spent three nights tearing up the floor in the shop and laying those gold bars in their place. They are all still there. That bitch has been walking on them since she bought the place." he glared at Rogers."Walking on them like they were just red brick."

"And Ruth?" Ed asked.

Jefferson laughed and rocked back in his chair. "She's there too." he finally said.

"Got her a solid gold urn and she's there in the shop, she deserves to be there." he shifted forward in his chair. "We forged metal in that shop so I know how to melt metal." he added. "Yep she's there in that kitchen." he added.

"Scott, we found the urn." Ed said. "Nice job with the urn." he added.

Jefferson lunged at Ed "You desturged my wife's eternal rest? he bellowed. "You son of a bitch."

Ed held his gaze. " You got anything else to tell us?" he asked.

Jefferson shook his head the anger still flashing in his eyes. "Guess not." he said

"Where's Charlie?" Derrek asked and Jefferson shifted his stare toward him

In New York. Works for that candy company, in shipping. Comes back to Heaven now and then" he added and smiled.

A knock came on the interigation room door. "Excuse me, there's a call for you Agent Hanson. You can take it down the hall on the first desk."

Ed got to his feet. "I'm done with this man." he said to Jefferson " Excuse me."

Derrek looked at Rogers who was fixed on Jefferson's face. "You coming Phil?" he asked.

Rogers got to his feet and turned to Jefferson. "Thank you for closing my last case. " he said and followed Derrek out the door.

Ed Hanson was perched on the corner of the desk listening to the voice at the other end.

"So what's her prognosis?" he asked as Derrek and Rogers approached.

"I see, that's great. We'll be in touch." he added hanging up the phone.

"Well?" Derrek asked

"That was Sandy's doctor. She's off the machines, and awake. Can't talk yet but he says she'll be fine."

The three men high fived and slapped each other on the back.

"You did it." Rogers said to Ed. "It's unbelievable but you did it."

Ed nodded. "Had a lot of help." he said sliding his arm around Derrek and Rogers shoulders.

"Gentlemen what say we go and mine some gold?"

EPILOGUE

Sandy Jessop set a double chocolate lava cake in the center of our kitchen table and smiled.

"Someone told me that chocolate is everyone's favorite." she said sitting down in the empty chair.

"How are you feeling?" I asked as she cut the cake and put the slices on plates.

"Almost normal." She said. "I get tired quicker than normal but the doctor says that will fade."

She passed the plates around the table. And leaned over to plant a kiss on Ed Hanson's cheek.

Ed turned a deep red and asked, "What's that for?" as she planted another kiss on Derrek.

"For saving my life and solving the mystery." She replied and took a bite of the cake.

"Okay," Helen said, focusing on Ed and Derrek. "We want to hear the entire story."

Derrek shoveled a hunk of cake in his mouth and swallowed. "Dang it woman, you sure know how to bake." he said to Sandy.

"Ed here put the pieces together in the middle of the night." Derrek said. "The pieces were there all along, but he managed to put the puzzle together."

Ed nodded. "It was the Heaven Fire Department's Investigation." he said and chewed cake. "The description of the body found in the train shop didn't seem to match up with the description we had of Scott Jefferson. It seemed to be shorter and heavier. But the coroner at the time attributed the discrepancy to fire damage. They never even considered it wasn't Jefferson."

Sandy shook her head. "All that gold hidden under my feet," she said. "How much did you recover?" she asked.

"Best estimate is about six million." Ed said. "We still have another section to get out." he finished the cake and swallowed coffee. "All told, I'm guessing about ten, twelve million." He added.

"When can I re open?" Sandy asked.

"Couple of weeks at best, possibly sooner." Ed replied, "Don't you think you'd better take it easy for awhile?" he asked.

Sandy smiled. "That doesn't pay my bills." She said. "I really need to get open again."

Derrek smiled. "Tell her the rest of it," he said to Ed grinning.

"Well, we've pieced the robbery together. The take we estimate was about six million based on the gold prices of the day. Today it's almost double." He added.

"With what Scott told us, they brought the gold back here, or at lease most of it. It was decided to replace the brick floor in the shop with the gold bars and paint over them. After that, they sent Charlie up to Harris and he actually went to school with you in your senior year."

"When Maynard Perkins started getting nervous and Scott felt he was a liability, Ruth bashed his head in and set the fire."

"Somewhere along the way, they decided that Scott would disappear and they would let the public assume that he was the body found in the rubble. Letting Ruth take the rap for arson was better than murder, because she was greedy, she filed an insurance claim. "

"She was convicted, and Charlie put on a great act over suing the village. I think he knew where his dad was the entire time. Scott and Charlie were living in an apartment on Main Street and they managed to go unnoticed all this time."

Sandy shook her head. "Okay, but why didn't he just get some of the gold and leave?" she asked

"Greed." Derrek said. "Maynard was dead, and Howard keeled over from a heart attack six months after the robbery. Clint was too afraid to look for the money, so that left all of it to Scott."

Sandy shook her head. "Then he or Charlie must have somehow scared off the tenants that rented the shop?" She asked.

"That's correct." Ed said. "He'd sneak into the place and take stuff or move things." He looked over at Helen.

"Your ghost theory was pretty close to what happened. The tenants would get scared and leave."

"And Charlie?" Hattie asked.

"We've got him in custody, and he should be back in Harris in a couple of days." Ed said. "We found him working in the shipping department of Elegant Design Sweets. He's the one that redirected the package of chocolates to Harris. Clint stole the poison from his workplace and laced the chocolates."

"And all because I spent some time with dad at the bank." Sandy said shaking her head. "That's a sick mind." she added.

"He'll go away for the rest of his life and Charlie will do some serious time." Derrek said. "But you shouldn't feel guilty." He told Sandy. "All you did was open a sweet shop. There was no way for you to know how reckless Scott Jefferson was, or how sick."

"Well,hopefuly I can pull out of the hole I'm going to be in." Sandy said leaning back and studing the crumbs on her plate.

"You will." Ed said. "In fact, I've got a surprize for you."

He pulled an envelope out of his pocket and handed it to her. "The bank in Del Mar is going to replace any damage to your shop, and they sent you this."

Sandy looked around the table and slowly opened the envelope. Her face went pale and her lip quivered.

"Oh my gosh!" she whispered. "I can't take this."

"You certainly can. It's the reward money from the robbery, with a little adjustment for inflation." Ed said, smiling. "You'll be able to do whatever you want. We all hope you stay here and reopen the shop." he added.

Tears rolled down her cheeks as we all hugged and I think Helen, Hattie and I cried a bit too.

Mark gave Sandy a big hug and said, "You better stay here. I'm addicted to those fudge brownies."

We all laughed and dished up seconds of the cake.

A week later, the gold had been removed, the floor repaired and Sandy was allowed back into the shop.

Ed Hanson stopped in to the Two Sisters a couple of days later.

"Ladies, it seems I'm always saying good bye," he said giving us a hug.

"You should stay." Helen told him."After all, why leave Heaven?" she added.

Hanson smiled "Maybe I'll be back." he added and picked up his breifcase. "Until then." he added and opened the door.

We watched as he crossed the street to Sandy's shop. A sign on the door announced, "Reopening soon."

As he disappeared inside, Helen turned to me and said. " I think Mr Hanson has a very good reason to return to heaven"

"A very sweet one, too." I added.

Made in the USA
Columbia, SC
22 October 2024

5640c1d9-72ae-4f4c-b8dc-c0c3eba40597R01